The Red Brick Road

The Red Brick Road

Text copyright © 2021 Levi Bronze

Email: levibronze45@gmail.com

www.levibronze.com

Illustrated by Margaret Williams

Cover Design by NX ARTS

All rights reserved

ISBN 978-0-578862-07-1

LCCN 2021903478

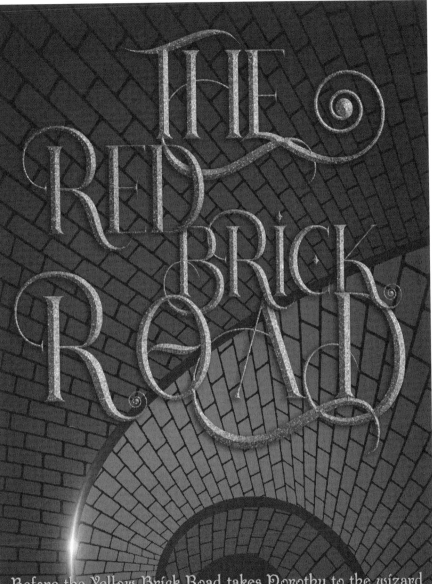

THE RED BRICK ROAD

Before the Yellow Brick Road takes Dorothy to the wizard
The Red Brick Road will push her to the edge

LEVI BRONZE

Acknowledgments

To Jena, my loving wife, strongest supporter, greatest encourager, and fiercest critic. Without you, my love, this book would have never come to fruition.

To my son, your simple question, "Dad, where does that red brick road go?" was the seed for this story.

To Carolina at Zambrano Publishing, thank you for coaching and guiding me through the publishing process.

To all my first readers, Kelley Hafner, Tracey Adkins, Jenny Cooper, Lisa Caton, Kay Smith Tippett, and Trudi LoPreto.

Table of Contents

Table of Contents

And so, with Toto trotting along soberly behind her, she started on her journey. There were several roads near by . . .

-L. Frank Baum

Chapter One

Like anyone from Kansas, Dorothy knew a thing or two about tornadoes. She knew they could pick up houses. But she never imagined that they could carry houses to another world—a world filled with odd creatures, peculiar plants, strange trees, little people called Munchkins who lived in a little village called Munchkinland . . . and witches. Bad ones and at least one good one. Dorothy's house had landed on a witch—a bad one who wore THE MOST dazzling slippers. She didn't wear them anymore though. The impact of Dorothy's house vanquished the evil spell caster. Now the slippers were on Dorothy's feet. What use does a dead witch have for pretty shoes?

Donned in sparkling footwear, Dorothy headed out to see the Wizard of Oz. She didn't know much about the wizard other than the fact that he, and he alone, could help her get back to Kansas. At least that's what the good witch had told her. "Follow the Yellow Brick Road," she'd said. "And it'll take you to the wizard." So, Dorothy took her advice. What other option did she have?

Now, Dorothy had no sooner reached the first bend of the Yellow Brick Road till she came to a lone fashion boutique on the outskirts of Munchkinland. The store's eye candy and romantic charm drew her like a magnet attracting a needle. With covetous eyes she gazed through the front window at the beautiful inventory on display. Silk gloves. Satin ribbons. Elegant hats. Ballroom dresses. Some with exotic flowers. Some with colorful feathers. Some with glittery stones.

Dorothy stepped inside to peruse.

A turquoise dress caught her attention. She ran her fingers through its ruffled lace then pulled it from the rack and held it close to her lean frame. "Oh, look at this one, Toto. It's like it was made to be worn with these amazing shoes. It's nicer than anything Molly Anne Brewster ever had," she said as she finger-combed her pigtails. She studied her reflection in the large mirror on the wall. The beautiful dress and her near perfect complexion didn't prevent her from focusing on the bridge of her nose. She wished it were a bit narrower. Dorothy was convinced that, were it not for the shape of her nose, she'd be heaped with ongoing compliments for having a pretty face. People back home were forever praising Molly Anne's fair face, especially when Dorothy was within earshot. Or, so it seemed. Not a day passed that Dorothy didn't wish to be prettier and more popular than her archrival. Dorothy was convinced that she'd be everything Molly Anne was and more if only Aunt Em and Uncle Henry owned a business in town like the Brewsters.

After a few spins to see how far the skirt would flare, she returned it to the rack and walked over to the hats. "Toto, this place is utterly fantastic. It has all a girl could want."

"ALL? Did you say ALL?" a man said.

Dorothy turned, caught off guard by the presence of another. He stood before her, his shiny black hair slicked back and groomed with a flawless part, the perfect lines of his manicured beard accenting his smooth, chiseled face.

Dorothy looked down at one of the hats and ran a finger along the edge of its brim. "Well, yes. I guess so. What more could a girl want?"

The man walked over to Dorothy.

"What more? Why, there's so much more . . . so very much more. Let your imagination run free!" He raised his hands upward, thrusting them open as if he were shooting light from his fingertips. "Muster up your every wish! Life's too short to deny yourself! Declare what you want!"

"Well . . . I WOULD like to have dresses as fine and as lovely as the kind Molly Anne wears. This old blue and white thing I have on is too plain for me. It's unworthy to be worn with these beautiful shoes I'm wearing," Dorothy said, tugging at the sides of her dress. "Same with all my other dresses, which aren't many at that."

"You see all these?" the man said while fanning a hand toward the glittering collection. "These are simple, modest dresses for the simple, modest people of Munchkinland. I have more in another territory not far from here where someone of your demanding taste can get a dress even grander than these."

The man pointed to Dorothy's shoes. "Ones more in keeping with those magnificent slippers you're wearing."

"Really? Dresses grander than these?" Dorothy said. "I can't imagine."

"Oh, yes. Ones that would make Molly Anne Brewster's best dresses look like used dish aprons or tattered house gowns."

"You can't be serious!"

The man clutched the black lapels of his burgundy jacket and swelled his chest. "I am indeed. Why, I can see you in one of them right now and Molly Anne standing next to you on the verge of fainting with envy. You'd like that, wouldn't you?"

"I certainly would."

The man cocked his chin and batted his eyelashes.

"Well, it can happen in this land I speak of."

"Where is this land?"

The man snapped his fingers and pointed at her. "I'll make a deal with you. I'll tell you if you tell me the things you desire in life."

Dorothy nodded. "Deal. I'd like to be beautiful. Everyday. So beautiful that people are forever asking to take my picture. And, girls get mad because their boyfriends are always looking at me."

"Absolutely. Why not? Anything else? Surely there's more."

"And, I'd like to be wealthy too. So wealthy I could buy anything I want. Beautiful dresses. Fabulous hats. A big mansion. Have butlers and maids. Anything. And eat meat every day if I choose.

I'm tired of eating beans and potatoes all the time and having meat only on Sundays."

The man leaned down and looked Dorothy in the eyes. "I couldn't agree with you more. The place I make mention of is a place where beauty and wealth are just waiting for you. All you have to do is go there and take it. Like grabbing a firefly on a dark night," he said and clinched a fist in the air.

"It sounds wonderful. Tell me where it is."

The man turned on his heels and paced away from Dorothy a few steps, the long tail of his suit coat swaying as he walked. He raised an index finger above his head.

"I assure you we'll get to that in a moment. But, for now, keep on wishing." He made a rolling motion with his hand. "Surely, being the girl from Kansas you are, you have aspirations that go beyond fancy dresses and a pile of money."

"How did you know I was from Kansas?"

The man turned back to her. He put one hand over his heart, stroked his hair with the other and grinned. "I know all kinds of things, but they'll keep for another day. Today is all about you. So, carry on with your wishing."

Dorothy thought for a moment then dropped her shoulders as if defeated.

"What? What? Why such a dreadful countenance?" asked the man.

Dorothy shook her head. "It's no use. No one or no place can give it to me."

"Well, you see now. That's where your thinking is all wrong," he said, shaking an index finger. "But I can understand. You've been told things that aren't true . . . well-meant by some well-meaning folks, I'm sure. But false, nonetheless. What you need is for someone to point out opportunities. Give you a little encouragement. And all your wishes will come true."

"You think so? You really think so?"

"I know so. It's my business to know so. I've been helping folks like you for longer than you've been alive. Believe me, I know a deserving soul the minute I lay eyes on one. And you, Dorothy, are as deserving as anyone I've ever met. So, don't quit dreaming now." He winked at her with one eye. "You're on a roll."

"How'd you know my name is Dorothy?"

The man gave a tight smile.

"It may seem crazy," Dorothy said. "But I'd like to be famous. So famous that everyone recognizes me wherever I go. Stand in line to see me up close and get my autograph."

The man pulled a stool from under a table and sat down on it facing Dorothy, his eyes changing like kaleidoscopes being turned. The pleasant fragrance of his cologne crept into her nostrils, his scent the same as Uncle Henry's at Sunday morning preaching.

"Listen, Dorothy. Now, you're talking," he said. "Power . . . there's nothing so grand as power. When you have it you can do anything you want. Be anything you want. Have everything you want."

He gazed up at the ceiling and began raising one hand slowly. "This place I speak of is where your star can rise to the heavens."

He lowered his hand and rested it on her shoulder. "Your only limitations will be those you put on yourself. The only things you'll miss out on will be those things you deprive yourself of. It's all up to you."

Dorothy stared for a moment at his hand touching her then looked back into his fantastic, captivating eyes. "This marvelous place you speak of, where is it?"

The man stood up and rubbed his chin. He leaned against a display counter and peered down at her.

"Before I tell you WHERE, you have to settle in your own mind the matter of HOW."

Dorothy reached down and picked up Toto.

"How? What do you mean by 'how'?" she said, holding the little dog close to her cheek.

The man drew down his eyebrows the way Dorothy had often seen Uncle Henry do when he was about to say something important. "I mean the place will not yield its bounty if you're not of the right frame of mind about things. You have to go about things in a very particular way."

Dorothy made a rolling motion with one hand. "I'm listening. Go on."

"You have to relinquish ALL the things you've been taught and start living your life by a singlular mindset—a simple, rigid motto." He crossed his arms in front of his stomach. "Until you adopt it fully, you're bound for a life of just enough and no more."

"I'm sick and tired of just enough and no more. And, I'll do whatever it takes to get what I want in life."

The man smiled. "Very well, then. Here it is. From this day onward tell yourself, '*Me first no matter the cost.*'"

Dorothy grimaced and jerked her head back. "That's all there is to it? Just tell myself that?"

The man sat back down on the stool and pulled in close to her face again. Toto growled at the man. Dorothy stroked the irritated dog's head in effort to calm him as the man continued.

"No, you have to follow it up with action. You have to tell yourself, then obey yourself. At times it'll be easy. Other times it'll be so hard it'll wrench you to the core of your being. You may get hurt and you may have to hurt others. Comes with success I'm afraid. But, if you'll stay faithful to the motto, you'll look up one day and find yourself possessing ALL your desires."

"I don't know. I've always been taught the opposite. You know. To put others first. That's what Aunt Em and Uncle Henry have taught me ever since I can remember. So have others."

"And those who've taught you, how much glamour and wealth and fame do they have?"

"Well, not much . . . really."

"Then such a philosophy hasn't benefited them, has it?"

The man's questions hit Dorothy like hammers. Everyone back in Kansas who'd told her to put others first just barely got by. None had all the things Dorothy desired. Most didn't even have some of the things. Perhaps the man had a point.

"But those who've been teaching me are good people," Dorothy said.

The man extended opened palms and shrugged his shoulders. "What is good?"

Dorothy felt her moral upbringing starting to fracture. She looked at the man. "What is good?" was a question she couldn't answer.

The man slapped his hands to his knees. "I don't doubt they care for you and want the best for you. They've simply been teaching you what was taught to them. It's an ongoing cycle of misery and discontent. 'Be good,' they say. 'Do good,' they say. Such proverbs and the like have kept many promising girls like you from the beauty, wealth and fame they've deserved. With my vast experience I can tell you with conviction that being good is overrated."

"Really?"

"Really. Besides, it's weak. Good is a servant's word. Forget about it. Erase it from your vocabulary. Achieving and acquiring are the things that really matter. They sway the world. They make legends. And they only come to those who live by the motto. Life goes on with two types of people: those who get what they deserve and those who miss out. I help determined people get what they deserve. The others," he said, making a backhanded wave in the air, "Well, they're just a waste of my time."

Dorothy wrestled to adapt to what the man was saying.

"I don't know, Mister."

The man rose from the stool and started busying himself with his merchandise.

"Maybe I was wrong about you. Maybe you're not ready for fineries and privileges and power." He shooed her off with one hand. "You be on your way back to Kansas now. I'm sure before too long you'll learn to be content with beans and potatoes and homemade dresses."

Toto began to growl at the man again. Dorothy rubbed her faithful pet and pondered.

She'd never heard such talk in all her life. But the man seemed to have a point. All those who'd been teaching her over the years had none of the things she wanted out of life. She didn't want to grow up and be like Aunt Em and Uncle Henry. Having to work from sun-up to sundown just to have enough money to barely get by. Being looked down on because you can afford a new pair of shoes but only once a year. Never invited to the ladies' society meetings because you live on a farm instead of in town like Molly Anne Brewster and her family. Marrying a man who wears dungarees and brogan boots instead of taylored suits and designer shoes. No, Dorothy was determined to have more and better.

She sat Toto down on the floor and walked over to the man. "No! I'm ready, I tell you. I'm ready. Me first no matter the cost. It's the motto I'll live by from this day forward."

The man grinned as he re-arranged a pair of gloves. "Okay, then. If your mind is made up?"

"It is. As made up as it's ever been about anything."

"Very well, then," he said. He motioned with a jerk of his head. "Come outside with me."

Dorothy followed the man out of the boutique, Toto walking next to her. The man stood on the Yellow Brick Road and spread his hands toward the horizon.

"What do you see? Cornfields? Forests? Hills? Valleys?"

"Yes," Dorothy said.

The man lowered his hands and put them on his hips. "Uh huh." He looked down at her. "Of course, you do." He lifted his eyes and peered into the distance. "But there are other things out there that you don't see. Things like disappointment. Struggle. Heartache. Broken dreams. Discouragement. Poverty. They're all out there too. Just waiting in disguise for any fool to come along. But, you're no such fool. Forget about this Yellow Brick Road. That witch who put you on this road is keeping you from your dreams. The Red Brick Road, on the other hand, is where all your dreams will come true. Take it instead." He bumped her shoulder with the back of his hand. "Go get what you deserve."

"It's the better road, huh?"

The man placed his hand on her shoulder again and fixed his eyes on hers. "It's to die for," he said, his voice breathy.

Dorothy maintained eye contact and nodded. "I think I'll get started immediately."

The man narrowed his eyelids. "I would if I were you."

"Can you tell me how to get to the Red Brick Road?"

The man's lips stretched into a grin. "My pleasure." He turned and pointed. "Go back the way you came. When you get to the other side of Munchkinland, you'll come to a bridge with a glass bottom. Walk across it and start living by the motto."

"Me first!" Dorothy said.

"No matter the cost," the man added, his words deliberate, his demeaner as heartless as a viper's.

Dorothy started back to the downtown district of Munckinland, Toto trotting along close to her ankles. She rounded the corner at the Munckinland Bank. Up ahead, in the middle of the town square, the good witch talked with the mayor and constable. The clip clap sound of the slippers on the Yellow Brick Road halted their conversation. The good witch looked toward Dorothy. "Why have you returned?"

"I've changed my mind. I'm taking the Red Brick Road instead."

The good witch shook her head. "Foolish. Foolish. You're making a tragic mistake."

Dorothy returned a contemptible look and kept up her purposeful stride. The good witch hurried over to Dorothy and walked along beside her.

"I must warn you," she said. "Once you cross the Sparkleberry River, the Yellow Brick Road will disappear and you'll have to take one of the other roads."

Dorothy kept walking.

"It's the most hazardous of all. I adjure you to reconsider for a road once chosen must be a road then taken," the good witch said. "I have your best in mind. I promise. Besides, you'll only delay your return to Kansas."

Dorothy stopped and thought. She looked down at the slippers. They seem to speak to her. Their shine and sparkle prompted her to think about all the nicer things she wanted but didn't have and would never have unless she charted a path far different than she'd been taught back in Kansas.

"No. My mind is made up. No need in trying to stop me."

The good witch returned a stiff *suit yourself* smile. The mayor and the constable arrived at the scene, both of them protesting.

"You two sound like the folks back home," Dorothy said. She looked down at her dog. Let's go, Toto." She resumed her traipse toward the bridge, feeling her pigtails tapping against her back as she walked.

Chapter Two

The heels of the slippers tapped on the bridge's glass bottom as Dorothy stepped. As she walked, she looked down and watched the multitudes of shiny fish swimming in the clear waters of Sparkleberry River. Flower blooms the size of dinner plates grew in the leafy arches on each side of the bridge. Hummingbirds busied themselves in the blooms, undeterred by Dorothy's presence.

"Choose wisely. Choose wisely," a voice chirped from across the bridge.

Dorothy cut a glance at the multicolored parrot perched on a branch of a chubby tree that grew on the edge of the river. Two of the tree's thick roots piped down the riverbank and into the flowing water. A green bullfrog, fat as a beach ball, with a brown derby hat resting atop his head, sat on one of the roots. The round looking glass propped over his right eye had a magnifying effect, causing him to appear to have one large eyeball partnered with a much smaller one.

"So true. So true," the bullfrog croaked, his lower jaw ballooning.

"Choose wisely. Choose wisely," the parrot repeated.

The glass bottom bridge connected the Main Street of Munchkinland on one side of Sparkleberry River to a well-worn cobblestone path on the other. At the end of the path stood a brick building. A large wooden sign on the front of the building read *Decision Depot*.

"No turning back now. No turning back now," the parrot cawed when Dorothy stepped off the bridge.

"Too late. Too late," the frog said.

Dorothy looked back. The glass bottom bridge had vanished and Sparkleberry River, now as wide as an ocean, stretched to the horizon. Munchkinland was no more.

"Through this door and your journey begins, Dorothy," came a voice.

Dorothy turned. A lean man dressed in a charcoal-colored suit and a bright red bowtie stood on the porch. His curly salt and pepper hair bushed out from under the edges of his round, flat top hat.

"Right this way," he said, motioning toward the green door.

Dorothy stood still, surprised by the man's personal greeting. "How do you know my name?"

The man stepped to the edge of the porch and motioned again. "Come. Come. No time for idle chitchat. The road of your choosing awaits you."

When Dorothy and Toto reached the building, she stooped down and looked at her loyal pet. "Don't worry, Toto." She rubbed the head of the trembling little dog. "Things are going to be fine. Just like the man said. All we have to do is go get all the things we deserve."

The man snapped his fingers. "If you please, little one. If you please."

Dorothy stood up and took a deep breath. *Me first whatever the cost*, she coached herself and ascended the steps. The man reached for the doorknob. As he opened the door, the sound of voices and commotion bellowed from inside.

Dorothy paused and looked at the man. "My word! What in the world is going on in there?"

"This is Decision Depot. The place where one and all embark on the road of their own decisions in the hopes of arriving at the destination of their greatest desires. All these people are getting ready to make their decisions and you must make yours too." He motioned with one hand. "Let's get a move on."

Dorothy stepped inside the crowded room. Toto followed close to her feet, his ears back and his tail curled between his hind legs.

Tall people. Short people. Fat people. Skinny people. Pale people. Dark people. People with hats. People with bonnets. People wearing dresses. People wearing pants. People with big hair. People with no hair. People with sharp chins. People with two chins. They filled the room and moved in two single file lines, chatting, laughing, asking questions, and telling stories to each other.

"Wisdom line to your left! Decision line to your right!" proclaimed a deep, baritone voice from overhead.

Dorothy looked up to see a Munchkin-sized man standing on a small balcony, a microphone in his hand. The brown mole on his bodacious nose stood out like a raisin against his milky skin. Two long front teeth protruded over his bottom lip. The man pulled a watch from the pocket of his vest. "Let's get a move on, folks. We'll be closing in less than an hour. I remind you this is Decision Depot. Not INDECISION Depot. So be decisive. Have your choices made before you get to the elevator. Those standing in line after closing time will have to wait till tomorrow to choose their roads."

Dorothy felt someone touch her elbow. She turned to see a perfect part in the middle of a head of black hair. A woman about the size of the man who stood on the balcony looked up at Dorothy. Her smile reinforced the kindness behind her dark green eyes. She wore white gloves on her tiny hands. With one hand raised she directed Dorothy to a line of people.

"This way to the wisdom line, milady," she said

"Wisdom line? What's the wisdom line for?"

"It's the line you stand in to see he who wears the white crown. He's just beyond the big, white door."

"Do I have to?"

The little woman patted Dorothy on the arm. "You'd never want to embark on your journey without seeing him first. He'll render unto you marvelous treasures that will help you arrive safely at your destination."

"Marvelous treasures, you say?"

"Yes, most marvelous indeed."

"Well, if he'll be giving me marvelous treasures, I'll be glad see him."

Dorothy looked in the direction the small woman pointed to. A line of people wound back and forth through the large room. It reminded Dorothy of the long lines people waited in to ride the best rides at the county fair. She hated waiting in those lines.

"Are all these people waiting to see the man with the white crown?" Dorothy asked.

"Yes. Every one."

"And I have to wait all the way here at the back of the line?"

Yes, milady. But the line moves quickly. Don't worry."

"Well, with all these people ahead of me, the best things will be gone by the time I get to see him. I'll get stuck with the stuff that no one else wanted. Could you please put me at the front of the line?"

The woman inhaled, a look of surprise on her face.

"Now, that wouldn't be very nice. It'll be your turn soon enough."

"I don't care about being—"

The woman walked away before Dorothy could get the word *nice* out of her mouth.

Dorothy eyed the long line once again. Me first whatever the cost. She stooped down to Toto.

"Stay close, Toto. I'm gonna try something."

Dorothy walked along the line of people, making her way towards the white door, the word *Wisdom* engraved on it in gold cursive. Most of the people in line remained engaged in their conversations, oblivious to Dorothy's scheme. One man, however, gave her a suspicious look as she pranced up to where he stood. He turned and pointed to the end of the line. "Missy, the line starts back there!"

"Oh, I'm not a traveler, sir. I'm a hostess. I was just counting the number of travelers. You're number forty-six. When I'm finished, might I get you something to drink or a biscuit perhaps?"

The man removed his porkpie hat. "Pardon me. I've shamed myself. I thought you were attempting to jump in line. I beg your forgiveness." He bowed his head to her.

"No worries. It's a busy day here at Decision Depot. We're just trying to make your wait as pleasant as possible."

"And a fine job you're doing. I must say. Thank you for your kind offer, but I had supper just before arriving."

"We do apologize for the wait. We're doing our best. If there's anything you need, just let me know." Dorothy gave a charming smile and moved on.

She'd lied. Just flat out lied to the man's face. He'd even offered an honorable apology but she'd persisted in her nasty scheme. Dorothy felt bad . . . but not too bad. It had worked and, in the moment, that's all she cared about. Besides, he shouldn't be so gullible. "Serves him right. It was his own fault," she told herself. *Me first whatever the cost* had worked.

Dorothy arrived at the front without further confrontation. A slumped-over elderly man waited for the door to open, his beard reaching almost to the floor. He leaned on his walking stick with one hand. With his other hand, he held a suitcase.

"How do you do, sir?" Dorothy said.

"I'm in a lot of pain." He strained to look Dorothy in the eyes as he spoke. "Have been for years. But, I hear there's a nurse in the land of the Blue Brick Road who specializes in remedying back ailments."

"For years, you say? How did you come to have such a plight?"

"Back when I was just a little older than you, I was standing on a street corner, waiting to cross. A stagecoach, pulled by six horses, came blasting down the road. A mother cradled her infant with one arm and held her little girl with her other hand. The little girl was rambunctious; I mean to tell you. She jerked away from her mother's grip and ran into the path of the oncoming horses. I jumped out in front of them and pushed the little girl away just in time. I was fast enough to get her out of the way, but not fast enough to get myself out of the way. One of the horses bowled me over as the team stampeded by. The back wheel of the wagon rolled over my spine and I've been all but crippled ever since."

Dorothy put her hand over her heart. "What a sad story!"

The man gave a firm nod. "I'd do the same thing all over again, given the situation. The mother would've been bereaved of her daughter."

"Well, I sure hope the nurse you've heard about is able to fix you."

"I'm very hopeful. I've traveled for three days to get to this point."

Dorothy examined the man and pondered how she might win his trust.

"Here, let me hold your suitcase for you till the door opens."

The man returned a slight grin and handed it to her. "You must be an angel."

The door turned slowly on its hinges. Radiant lights of a thousand colors flickered and glistened from inside. "He who wears the white crown will see you now," came a tender, female greeting from inside.

Dorothy placed one foot next to the old man's cane. When he started to walk through the door, she kicked the end of the cane and dropped the suitcase in front of his feet. The man tumbled. Dorothy picked up Toto and held him close.

"Oh, he's fallen! He's fallen! Someone help me! Please!" she cried out.

Dorothy's plea interrupted the conversation a man and his wife were having as they waited. In an instant, they turned their attention to the feeble man, consoling him and helping him up. The door began to close, and Dorothy slipped inside. *Me first whatever the cost* had worked again.

Chapter Three

The walls and ceiling of the Wisdom Room gleamed like a galaxy of stars on a prairie winter night. Dorothy sat Toto on the floor, the lights twinkling on the slippers. The radiant lights turned into fireflies and took flight. They converged behind, around and above the throne illuminating it. A man sat on the throne, his long hair and lengthy beard a brilliant white. Two rows of lights, like the borders of a runway created a path to his throne.

"Come, my child," he said. "A journey lies before you that is of no little significance."

His voice resonated. Dorothy felt it in the floor through the slippers. With bronze, boney hands he gripped the edges of the arms of the throne. The pearl ring on his right hand glowed like the moon in its fullness. Dorothy walked with trepidation toward the man, her eyes locked onto his. Blue beyond comparison and inescapable under his thick white brows.

"Who are you?" Dorothy said.

"I am known as the Wearer of the White Crown."

"But, you're not wearing a crown."

"I don't wear a crown of common thinking."

"You mean to tell me that you don't have a crown like a king or a queen?"

The man moved his hands to his lap and interlocked his fingers. "No. Nothing mined or made by man. Neither gold nor silver nor platinum. My crown is the white fleece that grows from my aged head."

Great. She'd gotten all excited about meeting a man she thought was royalty only to learn he's just an old man with white hair. What a let down.

The man looked down at Dorothy.

"You've exerted your will and utilized your wits to get here and now you're disappointed that I've no jeweled crown on my head. What a shame."

Who was this old man? He'd just read her mind and that made her uncomfortable.

"Well, be that as it may, a journey awaits you," he said. "So, which road do you choose?

"Red. And, I'd like to get an abundance of your marvelous treasures before I begin my trip."

The Wearer of the White Crown pressed his lips tightly and nodded.

"Hmm. You would, would you?"

"I certainly would."

"Well, the valuables I possess and bestow on travelers are not things you hold. The wealth I share is timeless and makes for successful journeys on the various roads in this world."

"If they're valuable and I can possess them and others can see me with them, I don't care how old they are," Dorothy said.

The old man raised an open hand just above his knee. "Now, now, Dorothy from Kansas. It seems to me that you don't understand the difference between treasures and treasures indeed."

Dorothy sighed. The old man was wasting her time.

The man looked down at Dorothy and took a deep breath. His firm lips gave way to a compassionate smile.

"Now, let's send you on your journey. I know that I shall disappoint you. But I hope that by the end of your journey you will have found those things you thought useless in the initial to be priceless in the final. I give you four traveling companions to assure you on your journey—four proverbs for wisdom and character. The first is—"

Dorothy thrust her hand on her hips. "Words? You mean to tell me that all you have to offer is words?"

"Words of insight put into practice yield priceless treasures," the Wearer of the White Crown said.

"But I want possessions. The kind of possessions that will make me beautiful and make others envious and jealous. Money. Clothes. Jewels. Stuff like that. I don't need words."

"Oh, but you do . . . far beyond what you realize."

"Do you give the kinds of things I want or not?"

The man shook his head. "I don't. Besides, such things would, in no way, benefit you on the Red Brick Road. However, just a small collection of words put into practice will prove themselves more valuable than the wealth of any noble."

"Oh, you're wasting my time. I'll be on my way. How do I get out of here?"

The man pointed to a door. Above it, an illumined sentence read, *A Road Once Chosen is a Road Then Taken.*

Dorothy reached down and picked up Toto. The hem of her dress flared out like a half-opened umbrella as she whipped around to leave. She considered the encounter to be useless and hoped the Red Brick Road proved to be everything the merchant said it would be.

The heels of the slippers clacked louder . . . much louder than was necessary as Dorothy marched toward the door. Shoulders squared. Never looking back. The door opened and she tramped through it.

. . . .

The stillness of the depot made Dorothy uneasy. The crowd of travelers stood in silence with their attention focused in the direction of the door marked *Wisdom.* Dorothy slowed her pace and studied the scene as she snaked her way through to the front of the decision line. The doorman stood next to the elevator, his eyes, as those of everyone else, fixed on whatever was taking place near the wisdom door.

Dorothy tapped him on the elbow. "What's going on over there?"

"Tragedy," he said, shaking his head. "A real tragedy. In all my years of working here, I've never seen it before until today."

"What? What?"

The doorman kept his gaze on the commotion. "A traveler has expired."

Dorothy's heart began to race. "Expired? What do you mean?"

The doorman looked down at her. "Dead, little lady. A traveler has died. It happened just a few minutes ago."

"But how?"

"No one really knows. One moment the traveler was standing in front of the wisdom door. The next moment he was on the floor. The ambulance team tried to revive him, but the traveler had already passed from this life."

Dorothy gasped and brought her hand to her mouth. Oh no. She didn't mean to . . . kill him.

"Please stand back!" someone shouted.

The crowd parted, making a clearing in the middle of the room. Dorothy pressed her way through to the edge of the open space. Two uniformed men pushed a gurney. A white sheet covered a corpse from head to foot. The men wheeled the gurney out the door. A third paramedic followed them carrying the dead man's walking stick and suitcase. The sound of voices began to rise again as distraught travelers re-gathered their faculties and resumed their agendas. With her head down, Dorothy cut her way through the people and back to the elevator, her steps slow, her eyes watery.

"I think you were next. Were you not?" the doorman said. He tugged on her dress sleeve. "Excuse me. Weren't you next?"

Dorothy looked up at him. "Oh, yes. Yes, I was."

"Let's be going then, though our hearts be heavy," he said and pressed a button on the wall.

The elevator door slid open and Dorothy walked inside, Toto following. She turned around and leaned against the back wall, staring into the crowd.

"Select your road. Be on with it. Others are waiting," the doorman said.

Dorothy reached for the panel of lit buttons. Various colors beamed at her. Blue. Green. Purple. Orange. Silver. Pink. Brown. And, the one that was to lead her to fame, fortune and power— the red one. She pressed it and the elevator engaged. As the door glided shut, Dorothy imagined herself to be a convict standing behind a closing prison cell. She sensed that she was changing. Falling downward. Crossing a great line. The elevator car began to descend. Dorothy felt like she was going down into hell.

What had she done? She never intended to kill anyone. Hurt someone? Okay . . . if necessary. But kill. No way. This was never part of the plan. The clothing merchant lied to her. Didn't he? Well, no . . . actually he didn't. He just never told her things would happen this way. He knew they would, but didn't tell her. No, that's not true either. He couldn't have known. Could he? Unless . . . unless he was . . . the devil! If he was, then she'd made a deal with the devil—the devil! Wait, this was crazy. He wasn't the devil. He was just a man selling dresses and hats and stuff. A successful businessman. He wanted to help her be successful too. That was all. Nothing more. And, the old man . . . who's to say she'd killed him. The couple that helped him probably dropped him and he hit his head. That could've happened. Or, maybe the man fell all by himself after they got him up. Fell and broke his stupid neck. That could've happened too. And another thing. It's possible he bumped his head against the door when it opened. Not paying attention. Old people do stuff like that all the time. Or, someone could've told him that the whole 'nurse on the Blue Brick Road who can fix crippled backs' was a big lie. The news upset him so much that it caused him to have a heart attack. That could've happened to the old fool too. Anyway, he could hardly get around. Couldn't have had too much longer to live. Besides, what kind of life can a man have if he can hardly walk or stand up straight? It was his own fault. If he would've just let that stupid brat get run over by the stagecoach, he wouldn't have been like he was. Trying to be good. Just like the merchant said. And, look what happened to him. Just goes to show that good IS overrated and weak. He was better off dead. So, even if Dorothy killed him, she did him a favor. *Me first whatever the cost.* Dorothy was getting the hang of it now. When the elevator delivered her to the Red Brick Road, she'd start winning.

Chapter Four

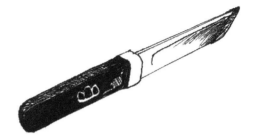

The elevator door opened. The low-lying fog crept inside and snuggled around Dorothy's ankles. She stepped to the threshold and looked out into the dimness. Toto began whimpering. Dorothy picked him up and held him close to her chest as the little creature shivered. "This is strange, Toto."

A bird cawed somewhere in the distance, loud and sharp. A wolf howled as if singing a solo in a horror choir. Then silence. An owl hooted from a nearby tree. Dorothy's eardrums registered her increased heartbeat. The man had tricked her. She stepped back inside elevator. She'd just select another road. She studied the panel of colored buttons. Blue. Yup. Blue. After all, the old man back at the depot said he was going there to see a nurse, so it was probably a good choice.

Dorothy pressed the blue button. The elevator doors didn't close. She pumped the button several more times.

"A road once chosen is a road then taken," said a gravelly voice from the speaker inside the elevator.

Dorothy jumped back against the wall and looked up at the disc of tiny holes where the sound came from. She gathered her wits. She'd try the green one. She pushed and held the button but the door didn't close.

"A road once chosen is a road then taken," said the voice again.

"No, no, no! I have changed my mind I tell you! I've changed my mind! The man tricked me! I'd rather just get back home to Kansas!"

Before she could press another button, the panel disappeared. The back wall of the elevator groaned and started lurching forward inch-by-inch, grating against the floor with a high-pitched whine. Like the jaws of a tightening vice, the space inside the elevator car grew smaller and smaller. The wall pressed up against Dorothy's back forcing her closer and closer to the door. The slippers slid on the floor of the elevator as if it were made of glass. Dorothy turned around and tried to push the wall back. Her effort proved useless as the unyielding wall continued to force her toward the dark, foggy terrain. Dorothy beat the wall with one hand as she held Toto with the other.

"No! Please! No! We don't want to take this road anymore! We've changed our minds! We've changed our minds!"

The texture of the wall changed, the once smooth surface now rough to Dorothy's fist.

The sudden change halted her fretting.

She took a step back and looked up. The elevator had transformed into a great tree.

"Scared. Are you?" said a voice from behind her.

Dorothy spun around.

A teenage boy wearing overalls leaned back against a large boulder. He looked to be a couple of years older than Dorothy. With one foot on the ground and the other against the base of the rock, he held a piece of wood over the top of his bent knee and whittled on it with a pocketknife. He smiled at Dorothy as he stroked the wood with the blade.

"No, I'm not scared. Just a little surprised maybe. But not scared."

The boy stopped whittling and inspected the wood. "Naw. A girl like you in a spooky place like this. You're scared. I can tell."

He cut another sliver out of the wood.

"Oh, you're just full of yourself."

He grinned and continued whittling.

"What are you making anyway?"

The boy stopped and looked Dorothy in the eyes. "Oh, just a little something for later."

He folded the pocketknife shut and shoved it into one of his front pant pockets, stuffing the wood in the other. With one hand he raked his thick blonde hair back. "So, why did you come here to Nimrod's Swamp?"

"I was tricked. At least I think I was. I started traveling on the yellow road. But I met a man who persuaded me to take this one."

"I see. Well, just how did he do that?"

Dorothy took a few steps toward him. "He told me this road is where all my dreams would come true."

She put Toto down. Raised her hands and looked around. "But judging from the looks of this place I'd say he lied to me." She dropped her hands. They slapped against her sides.

The boy folded his arms. "And what kind of dreams do you have?"

Dorothy wasn't ready to divulge such personal information. She was on the Red Brick Road in the middle of a swamp because she'd opened up to the boutique merchant. A total stranger. An impressive stranger no doubt, but a stranger nonetheless. She felt vulnerable enough already. She'd keep the conversation on the surface.

"Oh, it doesn't matter now," she said with a wave of her hand. "I need to just go with my original plan."

"Which is?"

"To get to the Emerald City. Have you heard of it?"

The boy interlocked his fingers behind his head and rested back against the bolder. "Yeah. I've been there."

"The good witch said the Wizard of Oz lives there. That he'll help me get back home to Kansas."

The boy chuckled. "The GOOD witch?"

"That's what she said."

The boy turned his head and looked at her. "And you believed her?"

Dorothy stared at the boy, not knowing what to say.

The boy prodded her again, this time his tone carried insult. "You did believe her, didn't you?"

"Well . . . ah . . . " She didn't have reason not to believe her. "The Munchkins vouched for her."

"Munchkins?"

"Yes. Odd, little people who live in Munchkinland."

Dorothy wished she'd not said "odd."

She offered clarification in an attempt to recover. "Odd is not the best way to describe them. I mean they're honest and wise."

The boy stood, put his hands in his pockets and paced toward her.

"So, let me get this straight. A witch that's good, a bunch of small, odd people and a wizard who can get you to a place called Kansas. Sounds like you'll fall for anything."

He stopped. Grinned, his eyebrows raised. "Hey, guess what? You see that mutt you're holding? I have a castle complete with knights and servants that I'll trade you for him." He started to laugh and hold his stomach. "And . . ." He tried to continue but his laughter wouldn't let him.

Toto barked as the boy bent over. Cackling. Dorothy felt small and stupid in his presence. She bit her bottom lip, feeling the heat in her cheeks.

"You're mean," she said. "And down right deplorable."

"And you . . . you are about as bright as a rusty can full of night crawlers if you ask me."

Dorothy raised one side of her lip. "Oh, I'm more intelligent than you any day, Swamp Boy. I bet you can't even spell the word *education*."

The boy's facial expression turned solemn. He raised himself up slowly, his blue eyes locked onto hers all the while. "Well, we'll just see about that. I tell you what. You ask me three questions. Any questions you wish. If I miss even one of them—game over and I take you to the Emerald City. If I answer all three, then you have to play MY game," he said and thumbed his chest. "And, you have to beat me at it before I'll take you there."

"And what if I refuse altogether?"

The boy shoved his hands back into his pockets and gave her a cool look. "Then I'll be on my way and you can fend for yourself the best you can. But I must warn you. This road can be terribly confusing to an outsider with its detours and forks and dead ends. And dangerous. Hoodlums and vile characters hide out beside it. Why do you think I carry a knife?" He started pacing around Dorothy and Toto. "So, what's it gonna be? Huh?" He pulled out the knife and the wood. With the flick of a wrist he opened the knife.

Dorothy began rolling over in her mind some of the various things she had learned in school. She'd always received high marks in every subject. There was no way the boy could know all the things she knew. As a matter of fact, she had her first question in mind already. Accomplishment, mingled with snobbish pride, and fear she'd never admit to made her decision an easy one.

"Okay, you're on."

The boy grinned and started nodding. "Yes! Now, that's what I was hoping you'd say. Let's begin. Shall we? Ask your first question."

Dorothy raised her eyebrows. "What's the Pythagorean Theorem?"

The boy winced as if suddenly plagued with a sharp pain. He stepped away from her, mumbling as he continued whittling on the wood. Then, he stopped and raised the open knife toward the gloomy sky. "I've got it. I've got it." He spun around on his heels, his face displaying a conceited smile. "A squared plus B squared equals C squared."

The boy's correct answer made Dorothy's heart flutter. How could he have gained such knowledge? Dorothy considered what her next question might be.

"One down. Only two left. Better make'em good ones," he said.

Dorothy rolled her eyes and waved him off. "Oh, everybody knows that one. I asked it so you wouldn't lose right off. This next one'll get ya."

"Okay. Let's have it then."

"In Greek mythology what separates the world of the living from the world of the dead?"

"Mmm. Greek mythology? Now, just what is Greek mythology?" he said into the sky as he tapped his cheek with the flat of the knife blade. "Can't say I've ever heard of that."

The boy folded the knife again and put it back in his pocket along with the block of wood. He walked over to a tree and broke off one of the branches. "Or, have I?"

He turned toward her, his eyebrows raised. "Yes. Yes, I think I have." He broke the branch in two pieces and held them up before her. "Look. One stick is now two sticks." The boy made a dramatic inhale and brought a hand to his mouth. "Oh, did I say sticks? Uh huh. I did. Didn't I? And there's the answer. The Styx River."

Dorothy thrust her head forward. "What! How do you know such things? You look miserably educated."

The boy tossed the sticks and smiled at her. "And just what does handsomely educated look like?"

Dorothy pondered what her last question might be. What could she ask him? Something that he could not POSSIBLY know.

The boy walked to the edge of the road and looked out into the dark swamp. "A woman lives not far from here. Endora's her name. As legend tells it, she was born without a tongue. Her parents didn't want her. Thought she was cursed. So, they brought her out here to this swamp one night and left her in a hollowed-out tree stump. She somehow survived." He turned and started walking back to her. "Her meal of choice is tongue soup. She hunts and catches whatever she can, cuts out the tongue and cooks it in her pot. That's why this swamp's so quiet most nights. Endora's soup-pot. So, you better hurry . . . whoever you are." The boy kicked a rock into the soggy forest and started whistling.

Her name. That was it. He didn't know her name.

Dorothy peered at him. She raised her eyebrows. "What's my name?"

The boy ceased his whistling. He gritted his teeth and scowled. "Now that's a dirty one. A genuinely dirty one."

Dorothy cracked a thin smile. She sensed victory. "You said I could ask you anything. And that's what I'm asking. A deal's a deal. Answer it and I'll play your game just like we agreed. And, if you can't, then you have to take me to the Wizard right now."

The boy raised a palm to her. "Okay. Okay. I may not be the most esteemed person in these parts, but no one can say that I ever reneged on a deal."

Dorothy looked down at the slippers. She moved one leg forward, raised her heel and twisted the toe of the shoe. "No rush. Take your time. Aren't these the most beautiful shoes you ever did see?"

The boy looked up into the treetops. "Now what might your name be? Something of royalty like Caroline or Elizabeth or Alexandra or Catherine? Something of nature like Rose or May or Daisy or Summer? Something of virtue, perhaps, like Hope or Faith or Joy or Charity?"

"You should see them in the sunlight," Dorothy said. "They sparkle and gleam."

"If I were to say any one of these wonderful names, you'd be more than pleased and I'd lose our little competition. Because none of them are right." The boy rubbed his chin. He walked over to her and leaned down. With his face only inches from hers, he looked her straight in the eyes. "Hm. Is it . . . Dorothy?"

Chapter Five

Dorothy stood in shock.

The boy turned and took a few steps. He lifted both hands to the sky, "Did you hear that, everybody? Her name is Dorothy and she has just lost even though she played dirty! Don't you feel sorry for her?"

He cupped one hand behind his ear. "I say, don't you feel sorry for her?"

The boy turned on his heels and walked back toward her. He fixed his eyes on hers and took one of her pigtails in his hand. "You know, I didn't hear so much as a frog croak or a cricket chirp. No one feels sorry for you and neither do I."

Dorothy wrestled to maintain an expressionless composure. The last thing she wanted was for the boy to derive any further satisfaction from how she felt. Out-matched. Lesser. Humiliated. At his mercy. And she hoped he had some mercy.

"Now, it's time to play my game. Follow me," he said and started walking down the road.

"Where're we going?"

"You'll see when we get there."

Dorothy stopped. "Well, what if I don't come with you?"

The boy paused and clicked his tongue, but didn't turn back. "You mean you're thinking about not playing my game after I've played yours?"

"Maybe."

The boy turned around. He leaned toward her and looked her in the eyes. "If you don't come with me, I'll pay Endora a visit. Tell her you're out here ALL alone, just you and your little dog. She'll have two tongues in her pot before daybreak. So, you decide, Dorothy."

He turned back around and started walking again.

Dorothy picked up her cherished friend and held him next to her cheek. "Toto, I think he's the most despicable human being I've ever met."

She started walking. "Okay, I'm coming. But, since you know my name, it's only right that I know yours."

"I'll tell you when my game's over." He glanced over his shoulder. "Maybe."

The boy pulled two large apples from a tree near the edge of the road. He turned and tossed one back to Dorothy. She waited until she heard him bite into his.

"Don't worry, its not poisonous," he said as he chewed.

She bit a large plug. Juice ran down her chin. Toto whined and licked her face.

"Toto's hungry too. What can he eat?"

"He's a dog. Put him down and he'll find something."

"But what if he strays too far? That wicked woman might get him."

The boy didn't answer. He just kept walking in the ankle-deep fog. A vine hung down from a low-hanging limb. Dorothy reached to push it away as she passed. The vine felt warm to her touch. It curled and clung to her arm.

In reflex, Dorothy turned her head to see the snake's half-opened mouth.

She let out a piercing scream. Toto barked. The boy looked back, then dashed toward her, pulling the knife out of his pocket as he ran.

He flipped the knife open with one hand. Grabbed the snake just below the head with the other. With a single stroke he decapitated the serpent and tossed its head to the side of the road. The remainder of the snake twisted and coiled in its blood on the red bricks.

"You better stay close to me," he said, wiping the blade with a large leaf from the tree. "It's pretty evident that you can't take care of yourself out here."

Dorothy stepped back from the wiggling, headless portion of the snake. "Oh, I wasn't scared. Just startled. That's all. I can take care of myself here or anywhere else."

The boy dropped his chin close to his chest and looked at Dorothy with raised eyebrows.

"You don't say."

"Yes. I do say."

"Well, I'm sure that you'll have opportunity to do just that and many times over by the time you reach the Wizard of Oz." He closed the knife and shoved it back into his pocket.

Dorothy walked beside him as they climbed hills and turned curves along the Red Brick Road. Crooked, gnarly tree limbs reached down over the road like the boney fingers of a multitude of grim reapers. When they came to a narrow bridge, the boy stopped and turned to her. "We have to go over one in front of the other. I'll go first. Make sure you hold to the ropes and watch your step. Some of the slats are out. If you fall, you're a goner. It's a long way down."

Dorothy rolled her eyes. Where was he taking her?

"And watch for Crag Lurchers. They own the bridge. The Nesterclop pays them a gold coin for every traveler they bring him."

The boy started across the bridge. Dorothy followed close behind, Toto in her arms. What was a Crag Lurcher? Who was the Nesterclop?

"And what does this Nesterclop do with the travelers?" Dorothy said.

"Some of them he eats," the boy said, mindful of his steps. "The ones he doesn't, he sells to the Molewiggins for gold. They live in the shafts of Darckbaal Mountain. All they do is dig, eat and sleep. Or so I'm told. I've never seen one, and from what I hear, I never want to." He paused. "Three boards are out right here. It's a wide gap, so don't try it, I'll help you." He leaped across then turned back and extended a hand to her.

Dorothy stepped to the edge of the gap. A board snapped under her foot. She jumped back and watched part of the plank fall down into the deep, jagged ravine. She considered stopping. Just forgetting the game. Turning around and doing the best she could on her own. But the notion of falling into the hands of a tongue-eating swamp woman convinced her otherwise.

She swallowed her pride and reached out her hand to the boy's.

His grip was warm and firm. As she leaped across the gap, she felt his strength as he lifted her to safety near where he stood. He released her hand then turned and resumed walking. Dorothy followed. As she approached the end of the bridge, the heel of one of the slippers hung in the crack between two of the boards. Dorothy fell forward. She screamed, dropping Toto as she crashed at the end of the walkway. The boy spun around and reached down to help her up.

Dorothy pushed his hand away. "Oh, just leave me alone! I'm fine! I don't need your help! I almost fell to my death because of you and your stupid game! My dog too." She stood up and straightened her dress. "What kind of game is your game anyway? I asked you three questions! And then you take me on a death march to who knows where."

"You did agree to the deal."

Dorothy waved him off with her hand. "Oh, whatever! Let's just get all this over with as soon as we can so I can get to the Emerald City. You repulse me. You think you're better than me but you're not. Okay, so you answered some questions. Big deal!"

The boy laid his hand on her shoulder.

"Trust me. I mean you no harm."

Dorothy shoved his hand away.

"Don't touch me! Don't even talk to me! Just go! The less you say to me the better!"

"Okay, fine. If that's how you want it. We'll just stick to our deal."

"That's exactly how I want it!"

The pale green moon glowed in the evening sky as the two traveled on the red bricks. As they came to a bend in the road a weathered sign pointed into the dense woods. The sign read *Devil's Spit Spot*.

The boy left the Red Brick Road and ventured in the direction the sign pointed. Dorothy followed, laboring through the undergrowth and under the tree limbs. After several steps the boy stopped and looked back.

"We're coming. We're coming," said Dorothy.

"You're too slow. It's getting dark. If you don't keep up, I'll leave you out here all by yourself. Then, you'll never see the Wizard of Oz and who knows what'll happen to you. So, you'd better keep up."

The boy continued to lead her deeper into the forest and further away from the Red Brick Road. Dorothy looked up into the blackness of the treetops, the moon no longer visible. The boy pulled out his knife again and cut several leafy branches. He bound them together on a stick with a vine he'd pulled.

He handed Dorothy the bundle. "Here, hold this."

Dorothy took it. "Okay. Sure."

The boy got down on his hands and knees and made a kindling pile out of some dry leaves and moss.

Dorothy watched the boy work. "What are you doing?"

The boy combed the top of the ground with his palms until he found a stone. He brushed some of the loose soil away and placed a handful of the kindling on top of it. He scraped the knife blade against the stone. The friction caused a spark. The boy leaned down low and blew into the kindling. A flame flickered and he added more from the pile. The blaze grew taller.

"Wow," Dorothy said.

The boy reached out his hand but didn't look up at her. "Hand it to me."

Dorothy handed him the bundle. The boy lit it, making a torch. She hated to admit it, but she felt safe in his care . . . almost.

"Okay. Let's go," he said as he raked some of the loose dirt over the burning kindling. He stood up, folded the knife into his pocket and hiked further into the woods. Toto whimpered as they walked. Dorothy rubbed him and kissed him in efforts to calm him, but the little dog remained anxious.

Dorothy caught the whiff of a foul odor. "Ew. What's that smell?"

She had no sooner asked her question when they came to a vast opening. The torch cast light on a spacious body of dark liquid.

"Is that what stinks so bad?"

The boy moved the torch around and examined the site. "Yup."

"What's this place called?"

"The Devil's Spit Spot."

"The Devil's Spit Spot? Why's it called that?"

The boy turned to her, his eyes gleaming in the torchlight. "Enough of the questions, Dorothy. You said you didn't want to talk to me. Remember? So, let's finish our agreement and be done with each other."

Dorothy felt the point of his sharp words. She nodded.

"My game's not a game of questions," he said. "It's a game of skill and concentration. It requires a couple of things."

The boy plunged the end of the torch into the bare, moist soil. He put his hands in his pockets. From one pocket he pulled out his knife. From the other he pulled out a small, pointed wooden peg. He held it up between his thumb and index finger. "I've been working on this just for you, Dorothy. The game is Mumbley-peg. Do you know how it's played?"

Dorothy smiled as if triumphant.

"Do I know how it's played?" she said and laughed. "Why I'm the best Mumbley-peg player in my whole school back home. You're gonna lose . . . whatever your name is. I'll stick the knife every time and I'll drive the peg so far in the ground you'll have to eat a handful of dirt to root it out."

The boy listened to Dorothy's arrogant discourse without giving even a single non-verbal cue. When she finished, he cocked his head and said, "Well, being that you are such a legendary Mumbley-peg player, you know that, if you don't go first, you don't get a turn until your opponent misses a throw. It's my game and I choose to go first."

Dorothy hoped he would miss. She had a hunch, however, that she'd just met her Mumbley-peg match.

Wasting no time, the boy dropped to his knees and, with the concentration of a surgeon, began flipping the knife. He started at his forehead and moved to his nose. Then, he flipped the knife from each ear. Next, his right shoulder followed by his left. Each time, the knife stuck half-blade in the ground. Dorothy looked on with apprehension as the boy worked the knife like he'd rehearsed it a thousand times. His skill proved flawless as he continued, flipping from each elbow, each wrist and each knuckle. Then, from each finger down to his final pinky. When he finished, he looked up a Dorothy. "Well, that's the full thirty-one sticks without a single miss. Looks like you have to root and you don't get a turn until you pull the peg. If you can't pull it, then game over. I win."

The boy pulled the knife from the ground, wiped each side of the blade on a pant leg. He held the wood peg erect at the surface of the ground. Point facing downward. Holding the knife by its opened blade, he raised the knife high to make the first blow. He brought it down hard on the blunt end of the peg, driving it into the ground. He repeated over and over again, each blow sending the peg deeper into the black soil. After he made the thirty-first and final strike, the top of the embedded peg was hardly visible. The once loose soil around it now smooth and patted down hard from the hammering of the thick case of the knife. In her quest of becoming the Mumbley-peg champ of her school, she'd rooted many pegs, but the one she had to extract now was the deepest and hardest driven she'd ever seen.

"Well, there it is, Dorothy. You gotta root it out or say uncle."

"Ain't as bad as it looks," she said, hoping to sound convincing and trying to psyche herself for the feat.

She put Toto on the ground, tied her pigtails behind her head and dropped to her knees.

"Remember, you can't use your hands. Just your nose and mouth," the boy said.

"I know the rules!" she said. She was hoping he didn't know THAT rule.

Dorothy stretched out on her belly and positioned her face over the peg. With her nose she attempted to plow the soil away from the head of it. Her nose scraped over the top of the hard dirt. The attempt proved futile. The boy had pounded the dirt around the peg into a firm crust.

"What's wrong, Champ? Having trouble? Nobody nose-plows when I drive a peg. I make the dirt as hard as slate rock. You're gonna have to use that haughty, big mouth of yours. It does a lot of big talking, but let's see if it can dig."

Dorothy didn't look up. "I've done it before and I'll do it again." She tried to sound confident. But the fact was, in the many times she'd played the game she'd never had to eat dirt. She'd made others do so on numerous occasions, but Dorothy had always either bested her competition or lost to someone who held back on driving a peg down below the ground's surface. The boy, however, had shown her no mercy. He'd given her the most difficult peg of all her experience. She opened wide and bit a full mouthful.

"Blah!" She spit out most of the dirt and gagged. She jumped to her feet. Bent over, she continued spitting and gagging. After a repetition of more than a dozen times, she had, at last, discharged enough of the dirt from her mouth so that she could speak.

"Ugh. It tastes like . . . I don't know what! It's ab-so-lute-ly horrible! I think I'm gonna be sick!" Dorothy put her hand on her stomach.

"Well, what's it gonna be? Are you gonna keep at it or say uncle?"

She coughed and spat again. "I can't do it. I just can't. Nobody could. Something's in the dirt that makes it vile. It's horrible, I tell you."

"Say it, then."

"Okay! Okay! Uncle!" She gagged and coughed and spat again. She brushed the dirt remnants from around her mouth and wiped her lips on a shoulder sleeve.

"I win, then. And, just what do you think I want for winning?"

"I don't have any idea. Just tell me."

The boy reached down and pulled the torch from the ground. "You'll see. Let's go."

Dorothy picked up Toto and followed the boy back into the woods. They came to a place in the forest where the thick ground foliage thinned to patches. Dry leaves crunched under their feet as they stepped. The boy walked to the base of a large tree. He cleared off a place on the ground and turned to Dorothy.

"We'll bed down here tonight. You'll find out what I get for winning when you wake up in the morning. Now, get some sleep. You're gonna need it."

The boy dropped the torch on a bare spot of ground and stomped it out with one foot. He didn't say another word. Darkness.

Dorothy couldn't even see her hand in front of her face. She put Toto down then curled in the fetal position on the forest floor. Toto licked the tears from her cheeks. She stroked his fur with one hand.

"What's he gonna want for winning, Toto?"

The faithful dog moved to her feet and lay down next to her ankles: his ritual sleeping place. Dorothy closed her eyes and then opened them. Just as dark either way.

Chapter Six

Dorothy stretched and rubbed her eyes to the sound of squirrels' daybreak frolicking in the branches above. She rubbed her arms with her palms to knock off the chill she'd garnered from the night. The sun hadn't risen high enough to conquer the defending cover of the trees' leaves. She reached over to give Toto the usual top-of-the-morning stroke on the head. Instead of fur, she touched cool soil.

She fanned her hand on the ground and sat up. "Toto!"

Nothing.

She jumped to her feet and scanned left and right. "Toto . . . Toto, come here!"

The woods seemed to be in a trance. Even with the low wind, the undergrowth remained perfectly still.

Dorothy turned to call in the opposite direction and then . . . she saw it. Where the boy had slept, a piece of paper flapped in the morning breeze. The game peg pinned it securely to the ground. Dorothy reached down and pulled it free. A note.

Dorothy,

I know what you did at Decision Depot.

Guilt pricked at her. How could the boy know what she'd done? He hadn't been at the depot, had he? No, he couldn't have been. She'd have noticed him. But there was no other way he could know. Was the boy a master of disguises? Was he much more than he appeared to be? Did he have super powers?

Dorothy's mind raced. Then, as if a giant stone had been dropped in her path, her thoughts halted. Toto was gone.

"No! No! No!" Dorothy cried out. "You didn't have to take Toto." The pain that only loss can inflict stabbed into her heart. Her throat tightened. She felt the water welling in her eyes. She rested her head on her forearm as she leaned against a tree. "Oh Toto. Toto." The tears rolled down her cheeks and dripped on her dress.

"Why are you crying? What's a Toto?" said a congenial voice from behind her.

Dorothy shot her eyes open and sniffled. "He's . . . he's my dog."

"I bet you'll find him."

She raised her head and turned to see the comforter. "You think so?"

A stag stood near the spot where she'd slept the night before, his head crowned with a symmetrical pair of antlers. Eight points on each side. When Dorothy made eye contact, the stag's white tail shot up. It bolted, its hindquarters jolting up and down as it darted into the forest and out of sight.

"Why'd you run away? I won't hurt you. I'm trying to get to the Emerald City," Dorothy said, a lump in her throat. "You spoke to me then you ran away. I don't understand."

Dorothy read the letter again then started walking, holding it with one hand at her side.

What kind of person would take away her dog? How did he manage to do it?

She dried her face with a shoulder sleeve.

"Maybe I can help?" a shrill voice said.

Dorothy looked around. No one in sight.

"I'm up here."

Dorothy glanced up. A creature sat on a limb with its back against the tree's trunk. It dangled one leg, the end of which had a four-toed foot with long, pointed nails. The creature smiled through ghastly, jagged teeth before jumping down. Dorothy stood still as he walked toward her, the end of his long tail rising just above the surface of the ground. Dorothy felt her blood cool in her veins.

"I can help you get your dog back AND get you to the Emerald City." He spread his hands apart. "I know every hill, moor, valley, and knoll in these parts."

Dorothy stepped back. "Uh . . . That's okay, Mister . . . ah?"

He broadened his smile. His teeth even more startling up close. "Skurtz." He gave a backhanded wave. "And leave off the mister."

Dorothy cleared her throat. "Well, Skurtz, what I was about to say is that I don't want to bother you in anyway. I'm sure I can find it myself."

He drew down his brow. "Nonsense. Count it a turn of good luck. I have a matter of business that takes me that way. Besides, I've helped scores of travelers journey to the Emerald City." He blinked his long eyelashes and raised his brow. "Shall we be on our way?"

Dorothy's mind reached for ideas. Just anything to avoid the repulsive creature's proposition. She feared making him angry. "Your offer is very kind, but I'm a young girl and, as such, I often need to take long rests when traveling. I'd slow you down. You wouldn't want to miss your appointment."

Skurtz frowned.

"And, I have an appetite. An appetite like you wouldn't imagine! Why I'm so hungry right now I'm feeling a little faint." She brought the back of her hand to her forehead. "So, I don't think it's a good idea to start on such a journey until I have some refreshment."

Skurtz opened his eyes wide and slapped a boney knee. "A dividend of good luck. You see, I specialize in acquiring tasty food. Close your eyes." He raised an index finger. "No peeky peeky."

Dorothy closed her eyes. What was he about to do? Rip her throat out? Summon a legion of others of his kind?

"Don't open till I say so."

Dorothy waited, her eyes clinched. Hopefully, he wasn't about to do something bad to her.

"Okay, you can open your eyes now."

Dorothy opened her eyes to find Skurtz now within an arm's distance. With his head bowed like a butler, he held forth a large platter. In the center sat a tall, frosty glass filled with water surrounded by various kinds of tiny sandwiches, desserts and fruits.

"Oh," Dorothy said. "Goodness. Everything looks delicious." She took a sandwich and shoved into her mouth. "I'm sorry if I sounded a little standoffish. But, I . . . oh well, it doesn't matter." She continued chewing and reached for a slice of fruit.

He raised his head and looked at her. "No need to say sorry. I understand. It can take some time for my congenial disposition to overcome my alarming appearance."

Dorothy swallowed the food. "Oh, I've hurt your feelings, haven't I? Please pardon me. I'm unfamiliar with your land and not at all sure whom I can trust. I'd be truly grateful if you'd help me get my dog back and take me to the Emerald City."

Skurtz's expression brightened, his smile so wide that dimples etched both cheeks. "It would be my pleasure. I didn't catch your name."

"Dorothy," she said and took the glass of water from the tray.

"Dorothy. Mmm. What a lovely name."

Dorothy took a few swallows of the water. She lowered the glass and wiped the corners of mouth with an index finger. "I'm from a place called Kansas. I came here for other reasons, but now I only want to get Toto back and then return home." She took a cookie from the plate and bit off a crispy bite. It crunched in her ears as she chewed. "I need to get to the Emerald City and see the Wizard of Oz. Do you know him?"

Skurtz narrowed his eyelids. "I'm sad to say I do."

Dorothy took a drink of water and chewed a couple times more. "I missed that. What'd you say?" She studied the remainder of the cookie. "I believe these are the best cookies I've ever had."

Skurtz raised his eyebrows and gave a tight-lipped smile. "Oh, I said 'I'm GLAD to say I do. When you're finished eating, we'll head that way."

Dorothy crammed the remaining portion of the cookie into her mouth and took another drink. "I think that'll do it for me." She sat the near empty glass back on the tray and dried her hands on the bottom of her dress.

Skurtz walked over to a nearby tree. "I'll just set this over here. I'm sure it'll strengthen some other hungry traveler on their journey." He sat the platter down and turned to Dorothy. "Now, Dorothy, the Emerald City is this way." He pointed and started walking. Dorothy followed.

The sound of whoo whoo whoo came from high in the trees. Dorothy looked up as she walked. A white owl sat perched on a limb, his large blue eyes gleaming. Dorothy felt as though the owl peered into her soul. She paused. The bird made a long blink then flew away.

"Come on. What are you waiting for?" Skurtz said.

Dorothy refocused her attention and trotted to catch up with him. "I have reason to believe that a mean boy stole my dog. I plan to get him back. Maybe we'll catch up to them along the way."

"Mm. A mean boy you say?"

"Yes, a very mean boy. What kind of person steals someone's dog?"

Skurtz turned and looked at her. "A mean one indeed. What's this boy's name?"

"He didn't tell me." Dorothy held up a flattened palm higher than her head. "He's about this tall. He's got blonde hair down to his shoulders, wears blue jean overalls and is always whittling with a pocketknife. Have you ever met him?"

Skurtz grinned a bit. "No. I can't say I have. But a boy who carries a knife sounds like an interesting boy to me."

Dorothy stepped in haste to keep up with Skurtz, routinely looking down at the road and back up to him as they walked. "He's not interesting at all. He tricks people is what he does. And he thinks he knows everything. I'm determined to find him and get my dog back. Then, I'm going to see the Wizard of Oz so I can get back home and I'm never coming back to this place. Everyone here's a liar."

Skurtz stopped and turned to her. "You say you'd like to get your dog back?"

"Yes, for certain. I've had Toto since he was a pup. I just can't go home without him. I bet he's missing me something awful right now."

Skurtz's eyes lit up. "Once again, Dorothy, you're the luckier for our acquaintance. I know someone who specializes in acquiring lost valuables. Your Toto is valuable to you, is he?"

"He's the most valuable thing I possess. I wouldn't trade'em for a satchel full of gold coins."

"That's some kind of valuable. A satchel full of gold coins is a sizable fortune."

"How long will it take for us to get to where your friend lives?"

Skurtz cocked his head. "Oh, I'd say we could be there before it gets dark. No problem. That is, IF we're determined and have no delays."

"I'm determined. As determined as I've ever been about anything. Besides, I don't foresee any delays. Certainly not for food. I'm as full as can be. Thanks to you."

Skurtz shrugged his shoulders and turned his palms upward. "Well, that's just the way I am, Dorothy. Always ready to be of service to those with potential."

"Potential?"

Skurtz stopped and touched her on one shoulder. "I see potential in you from your head to your feet."

Dorothy smiled. "Well, that's the most encouraging thing I've heard since I left Munchkinland."

Skurtz curled up one side of his lip and resumed the pace. "I never cared much for Munchkinland. Never really fit in. Munchkins can be crafty little creatures. You gotta keep your eye on them." He shook his head. "I don't trust'em. No sir."

Dorothy bumped him on the arm with the back of her hand. "How do you know about Munchkinland?"

He looked down at the place where her flesh had touched his. Smiled. Then focused again on the road ahead. "I used to live there. I felt judged all the time. It wasn't for me, so I picked up and moved here."

Several hours passed and the wooded landscape changed as Dorothy followed Skurtz. She talked briefly about the people back home she liked—Uncle Henry, Aunt Em, her cousin Isla Pernigan. She talked at length about the one person she liked the most—herself—of course. She noted for him all of her strong points, achievements and betterments. And, she spent ample time criticizing all the people who didn't measure up to her standards.

Skurtz listened and commented from time to time, but didn't divulge any information about himself. As they tromped along, birds chirped in a fuss and flew from the trees. A lavender bull elephant grazed among the low-hanging tree branches, his herd occupied with the same activity. He paused and looked at Dorothy and Skurtz. He peaked his ears and raised his trunk high above his massive tusk, "Uurruuhhn." Each member of the herd stopped its eating and stampeded away, the bull following like a guardian.

"Have you noticed how the birds and animals seem to be afraid of us?" Dorothy said.

"It's your long hair," Skurtz said.

"My long hair?"

"Yeah. Endora has long hair. You remind them of her."

"The boy told me about her. How much further till we get to where your friend lives?"

Skurtz opened his mouth, but a voice cut him off before he could speak.

"Help! Help! Somebody, help me! Please!"

They stopped and listened.

"Please! Help me, somebody!"

"It came from that direction," Skurtz said, pointing.

The two of them hiked through the thick trees, "Help! Help" getting louder the farther they walked.

Dorothy pointed. "There. Something's moving on the ground up ahead."

She and Skurtz rushed through the forest. Dorothy kept her eyes on the movement.

A female creature struggled to emerge from a mud bog, the soupy earth up to her shoulders.

"Don't let her see you just yet," Skurtz said. He grabbed a sleeve of Dorothy's dress and pulled her behind a tree. "It's a Gem-fairy. She's fallen into a Treetroll's quagmire." He looked around the trunk of the tree then pulled his head back quickly.

"Shouldn't we find a long branch and pull her out?"

Skurtz raised a hand. "Let's consider this opportunity."

"What?"

"Look on her hand."

Dorothy peeked around the tree and looked. On one hand, the Gem-fairy wore a gold ring. The large red stone inlaid in the ring pulsated as if a flame blazed inside it.

Dorothy pulled her head back and looked at Skurtz. "Okay. What about it?"

"It's a heartstone. Very rare. Every Gem-fairy wears one. That's why they're called Gem-fairies. It's worth a fortune. I've seen only two or three in my lifetime. None were as big as the one on her finger. She must be the Gem-fairy princess."

"A princess? Really?"

"Yes. The very daughter of the Gem-fairy king himself." Skurtz nudged Dorothy on the arm with the back of his hand. "I say we take it."

Dorothy drew down her brow and opened her mouth as if she'd just tasted something foul. "What? We can't do that to her!"

"When it comes to ruthlessness and brutality, Gem-fairies have no peer. Scores of innocent beings have perished at their hands." Skurtz put his hands on Dorothy's shoulders and pulled her face in close to his. "With that ring, we could buy up most of the Emerald City. You and I could be regents, prime ministers even. We'd be more powerful and renown than the Wizard of Oz himself."

The talk of power trickled in Dorothy's ear and down into her heart. It found the pride seed that had been sown there by the convincing merchant. And when it found it, it watered it. Her imagination blazed. She envisioned herself ruling in the Emerald City. People bowing down to her. Asking her permission. She imagined closets full of beautiful dresses. Chests full of sparkling jewelry. Vaults full of gold money. Make-up. Perfumes. Carriages transporting her around and people shouting her name in celebration. Toto at her side, of course. And the boy banished to a remote island or locked away in some dark prison.

Dorothy cooled her expression. "Okay, I'm game."

"Good, Dorothy. Good. Now, here's the thing. She'd rather die than accept help from me. Gem-fairies despise me and my kind. If I go near her, she'll kill me in my tracks." Skurtz peaked his eyebrows. "But you . . . well."

The Gem-fairy's misfortune was a great opportunity. It mustn't be squandered. Mustn't be fumbled away by succumbing to the weakness of pity. Dorothy had to do this. She had to dig down and do what was best for her. Hard as it might be. *Me first whatever the cost.*

"She's in a desperate situation," Dorothy said. "I bet I can get her to trust me. You just hide here and watch."

She stepped out from among the trees and took apprehensive paces up to the edge of the bog.

"I heard you calling for help," Dorothy said.

The Gem-fairy looked up at Dorothy. "No! No! Leave me alone! You're treacherous. I can tell from looking at your face."

Dorothy shook her head, fanning her hands. "No, I'm just a lost girl from a place called Kansas. I'm trying desperately to get to the Wizard of Oz so he can help me get back home. Do you know the wizard?"

The Gem-fairy continued to gaze at Dorothy's face.

"Maybe we could help each other," Dorothy said. "Do you know how to get to the Emerald City?"

The Gem-fairy nodded, the mud now at her neck.

"Okay. Think about it. You need help and so do I. I'll help you out of the pit and you can help me get to the wizard. What do you say?"

The Gem-fairy pressed her lips together. Inhaled then exhaled.

"I must admit I've never seen anyone like you before and I've never heard of a land called Kansas. You definitely aren't from around here so you must be lost. How'd you get here in the first place?"

Dorothy smiled. "It's a long story. I'll tell you on the way. Let me just find a long branch and I'll have you out in no time."

Dorothy searched the area around the bog and found a dry branch. "Here, I found one." She measured a distance the length of her arm and cracked the branch at the place level with her wrist. She rushed back over to the edge of the quicksand and extended the branch. With the mud now up to her chin, the Gem-fairy grabbed the end of the stick. Dorothy began to heave. Hand over hand Dorothy pulled the Gem-fairy closer and closer to the edge. When she felt the crack on the limb, she lifted up on it causing the stick to break in two pieces.

"Agh!" the Gem-fairy cried out.

Could Dorothy do this? Take her ring and leave her here to drown in the mud? The princess didn't seem like a treacherous killer.

Dorothy tossed her portion of the branch aside. "Don't worry. I've got you." She dropped to her stomach and stretched out her hands. "Here, give me your hands."

The Gem-fairy reached her ringless hand to Dorothy. With counterfeit effort, Dorothy grunted and pulled then let the Gem-fairy's hand slip from hers.

"Both hands! Give me both hands! The mud is slippery!"

The Gem-fairy extended the other hand. Dorothy grabbed her at the wrist and began pulling her closer to the bank.

The princess was small and pretty. She didn't seem ruthless or deadly. Maybe Dorothy should rescue her after all. Wait a minute. The boy. He was attractive and charming. And he'd tricked her. Then stole Toto. He was a phony. The Gem-fairy was probably a phony too. Why not take the ring? She didn't deserve to have it. Why help her? She deserved to die anyway.

Dorothy let her hands slide down to the princess's fingers. When her hand touched the heartstone, she gripped the Gem-fairy's ring finger like a cow udder and stripped off the ring. She released the princess's other hand and jumped to her feet.

"No! No! You deceived me!" the Gem-fairy princess said.

Dorothy slipped the ring on her finger and studied it. She rotated her hand and watched the heartstone gleam. Remarkable. Enchanting. So much so that its beauty deafened her momentarily to the princess's wailing. She gloried that the ring was now on her finger. If only the folks back in Kansas could see her with it. Molly Anne Brewster would be so jealous. No one possessed such an exquisite piece of jewelry. Not even the bank president's wife. Like touching a bare electrical wire the reality of what she was about to do jerked her back to the situation at hand. She looked down at the languishing heiress whose dainty nose was about to be submerged in the liquid dirt. Could Dorothy do it? Could she turn her back on her and ease back into the forest? She recalled the merchant's counsel. *Me first whatever the cost.* Did she want beauty, fame and power at this high price? Dorothy thought about it. Then, she slipped the ring off her finger. Dropped it in the pocket of her dress. And walked away.

Skurtz shot Dorothy a broad, gnarley grin. "Absolutely stupendous. You're a natural." He fell in behind her as she walked past him.

Dorothy stepped through the woods. Reflecting. The guilt of her fiendish deed began stabbing into her fledging conscience. The action felt dirty. She felt dirty. Felt herself changing . . . learning . . . growing dark in a way. She paused and propped against a tree. Stomach churning. Food rushed up from her stomach and she vomited.

"Are you okay?" Skurtz said.

Dorothy leaned her head against her forearm. "I'm not sure. I've never done anything like that before. Maybe I should go back. I might still be able to save her. Then I'll give her the ring back."

Skurtz placed his hand on her shoulder. "You don't know what you're saying. Gem-fairies are one of the great nemeses to this land. They've executed scores of my kin. You just performed a beneficial deed."

Dorothy heaved and gagged again.

"Really, Dorothy. You were absolutely incredible back there. It was amazing to watch. You're really a hero."

Hero? Dorothy didn't feel like a hero. She felt like a thief. Like a murderer.

Skurtz tapped her on the back. She raised her head and looked at him.

"Trust in the end results," he said. "Not feelings. What you just did prospered you, me and others as well."

Dorothy wiped her eyes. "I know that you and I now have the ring. That's a benefit to us, but what's the benefit to others?"

"Once again, it's good that I found you. I can help you think clearly. I think you'll make a most effective queen." He took his tail in one hand and pointed the end of it at her. "Do you think you'll make an effective queen?"

"Yeah, I guess so."

"No. You gotta be more confident than 'I guess so.' I'll ask you again." He held his tail firmly in his hand and tapped Dorothy in the middle of her chest with the end of it. "Do you think you'll make an effective queen?"

Dorothy liked the way this was going.

She nodded. "Yes. I believe I will."

Skurtz smiled, his eyelids narrow. "That's more like it. When we get to the Emerald City, you'll no doubt become the queen. And, as queen you'll be a huge benefit to all the citizens there."

Dorothy pushed up her top lip and squinted. "Mmm. Never thought about that. Does stand to reason, doesn't it?"

Skurtz stood up. He swung the end of his tail in a circle as though it were a chain. "It certainly does. Not to mention the fact that everyone around here will have one less Gem-fairy to worry about."

Dorothy cocked her head, now inspired with new confidence. "How much further till we reach this friend of yours who can get Toto back for me?"

Skurtz grinned and released his tail. "As a matter fact, it's not very far from here. Let's go."

He began walking, Dorothy following. They stepped out of the forest and onto the Red Brick Road. Dorothy hesitated and looked both ways. "Funny. I could swear I've been here before."

Skurtz motioned with his hand. "My friend lives just around the corner here."

Dorothy walked behind him. When they rounded the curve, she saw it. The bridge she'd crossed with the boy the day before. She stopped. "Do we have to go across it?"

Skurtz paused and looked back at her. "Yes. It's the only way."

"I crossed this bridge yesterday with the boy who stole my dog. He said terrible beings called Crag Lurchers live under it. Said they catch those who cross the bridge. Eat the ones they keep and trade the others to something called the Nesterclop."

"And you believed him? You're too smart to fall for that. Why, that ludicrous tale has been told and retold for as long as I can remember. Crag Lurchers. The Nesterclop." He shook his head. "All foolish legends. Just a bunch of slackerdrool and bumblegulch. Come on. The sooner we get across the sooner you'll get your dog back." He motioned for her to follow him and started across.

Dorothy considered the fact that she didn't see any the day before when they crossed. The boy abandoned her. And, she was certain that he'd taken Toto. SO, he must have been trying to scare her with all his talk about Crag Lurchers and the Nesterclop. Yes, that was it. Just like Skurtz said. It was all a bunch slackerdrool and bumblegulch. Whatever those were.

Dorothy took a deep breath and let it out. "You're right. I'm too smart to believe such a story."

She walked behind him as they traversed the bridge.

Skurtz looked back at her.

"I'm coming," Dorothy said.

She looked down into the deep gorge. Wait! What was that? Movement along the side of the ravine. Dorothy cut a look at it. Three chubby creatures pulled themselves up with speed and agility.

Dorothy clinched the railing. "Skurtz!"

"Sooo, Skurtz, what's this you've brought me today?" a voice said.

Dorothy whirled around to see a short, portly creature standing at the end of the bridge, a broad sword sheathed at his side. He stood upright on webbed feet, his viper-like eyes bulging.

"This is your best yet," he said.

Dorothy took a step back. "You stay away from me."

"She's from a domain far from here called Kansas," Skurtz said, glancing at her. "Egscar, I'd say the Nesterclop will pay a hundred gold coins for her."

Egscar ran his tongue across his pointed teeth. "She does look tasty. Even with Devil's Spit on her face."

"Devil's Spit? What do you mean?" Dorothy said.

Egscar started walking toward her. "Have you not seen yourself? Didn't Skurtz tell you?"

Dorothy turned and looked at Skurtz. He gave her a cool expression in reply and shrugged his shoulders. Then, it hit Dorothy like a brick. She leaned back against the rail of the bridge. The Mumbley-peg game. She must've gotten it from the Mumbley-peg game. That's why the boy took her there to play it. She licked a palm and started rubbing her mouth franticly.

"You're wasting your time. It'll take much more than that to get it off," Egscar said.

Dorothy looked back toward Skurtz. "I trusted you!"

Skurtz yawned and rolled his eyes. Three other Crag Lurchers now stood behind him on the bridge.

"So, it's true. These are Crag Lurchers. Aren't they?"

Skurtz inspected the fingernails on one of his hands. "You ARE a smart one, Dorothy." He looked at Egscar. "Let's stop wasting time. Do we have a deal or not?"

Egscar stroked his chin, nodding. "Oh, I want her. I want her. No question about that."

Skurtz lifted his tail to the palm of his hand and started twirling it as he walked toward Dorothy and Egscar. "Okay, but she's gonna cost you more than just your ordinary vacant cave. After all, she IS one of a kind."

"What did you have in mind?" Egscar said.

Skurtz dropped his tail and sprang to the top of the bridge's railing. He looked over the gorge and spread his hands apart as if he were parting the sky. "I want a prominent cave. One that will be the envy of all my fellow Scaithes."

"You lied to me," Dorothy said.

Skurtz jumped back down to the walkway and drew in close to Dorothy's face. "You call it a lie. I call it a shrewd maneuver."

"You're detestable," Dorothy said.

Skurtz rolled his eyes again and shook his head. "Birds of a feather you and I, Dorothy. Birds of a feather." He walked past her. "So, Egscar, do we have a deal?"

Egscar rubbed his chin and squinted an eye. "Mmm . . . a prominent cave, huh." He folded his arms and looked up into the sky. "Okay . . . done."

Skurtz clapped his hands once. "Very good. Now, where's the cave? And, you better not deceive me or I'll tell Endora where you sleep at night. Even you are no match for her. She'd love to have that fine tongue of yours in her pot."

Egscar swallowed hard. "If ah . . . if you go to Rantoul Grove you'll see a tree that grows to the northwest horizon toward the Emerald City. The tree has two large roots that overlap each other. The gap between the roots is the cave's opening. The cave has no equal in all the land."

"I can't believe you're gonna trade me to these Crag Lurchers for a cave," Dorothy said. "We could've ruled the Emerald City."

"We're wasting time here." Egscar said. "Let's make our transaction and be done with it." He turned to the three other Crag Lurchers. "Chains!"

Skurtz raised a firm hand. "Not just yet. I have a little matter to settle before you take her away."

"What would that be?" Egscar said.

"Never you mind. This'll only take a moment."

Skurtz walked back to Dorothy and leaned in close. "I'll be taking the ring. Our partnership is no more."

Dorothy spat in his face. He wiped it off then licked it from his fingers. "Not bad. The Nesterclop will love dining on you." He reached into the pocket of Dorothy's dress. "Might it be in here?" He fisted it and winked.

"I'll get it back," she said through gritted teeth. "And when I do, I'll—"

Skurtz pulled the ring from Dorothy's pocket, keeping his hand closed in order to conceal it. "Always the killer at heart. Atta girl." He looked back at Egscar and shrugged his shoulders. "Oh, well. I guess it got lost along the way. Now you can have her."

Skurtz leaned back against the railing.

Egscar tossed a ring of two keys toward the three Crag Lurchers. The tallest caught the keys. He walked up to Dorothy and began fastening a shackle around her neck.

What! He was going to put rusty iron around her neck! Dorothy tightened her jaws as the Crag Lurcher fastened the weighty collar.

The two smaller Crag Lurchers approached Dorothy, each holding a chain with an iron bond at one end.

As if shackling her neck wasn't enough.

Using one of the keys, the tallest locked the bonds on Dorothy's wrists then pitched them back to Egscar.

"Good doing business with you, Egscar. I hope I never see your toadish face again . . . ever," Skurtz said.

Egscar threw a look at Skurtz and raised one side of his mouth in scorn. "I hope some day you end up in the bottom of the black lake."

A bird-sized dragonfly landed on the bridge six feet away from Egscar. He shot out his tongue and snatched it into his mouth. He crunched it between his teeth a few times and swallowed it. "Let's go," he said and started walking toward one end of the bridge. The three other Crag Lurchers began ushering Dorothy, the chains clanging as the four of them walked. Dorothy turned her head to leer at Skurtz. He wasn't there.

"Whoo who," came the familiar sound. Dorothy looked up. The white owl sat perched in a tree above. It made a calculated blink with its large blue eyes and took flight. The tall Crag Lurcher tightened the chain, tugging Dorothy forward. She submitted and picked up the pace.

Chapter Seven

Dorothy walked the beaten trail along the edge of the gorge, the tall Crag Lurcher ahead of her, the two others behind her with Egscar leading the way. Dorothy fought back the urge to cry, determined to stay alert. *Be on the lookout for an opportunity to escape*, she told herself. Though Egscar had a hobble in his stride, he did have a sword and a brutal disposition. She'd keep her distance from him as best she could. She thought about the key that swung at his belt as he walked. How to get it?

What exactly the other three Lurchers could do was a question. They looked different. Their eyes made them seem . . . not so dangerous. The tall one was their superior, no doubt . . . he looked older, more competent.

Dorothy looked back at the two underlings. She wondered how they'd incurred the scars on their faces. War wounds? Fierce animals? One had fiery red hair that parted in the middle of his head. Dorothy gazed at him, but this didn't alter his somber expression. He marched, holding the chain as if under a spell. She made contact with the other one. His yellow hair stood straight up like a hedgehog's coat. He cut a glance up at her then quickly looked back down.

They continued on the pathway as it snaked along the brim of a deep gorge. Up ahead, a wall of stone rose from the bottom of the gorge as if a giant spade from the sky had plunged into the ground and hulled out the canyon. A one-time waterfall. A gigantic tree extended a massive bough over the ravine. Underneath it a railed wooden deck jutted out from the top of the canyon wall. Egscar stepped onto the deck and looked back at them. "Get a move on!"

Without breaking stride, the tall one looked over his shoulder at Dorothy as they walked and gave the chain a gentle tug. Dorothy moved faster. Egscar waited while Dorothy and the three Crag Lurchers loaded. Dorothy boarded the rudimentary structure and looked down into the bottom of the ravine. A dry riverbed weaved through the bottom of the canyon like a giant gash in the rocky terrain.

"*Gawaaaah!*" Egscar yelled below.

A swarm of Crag Lurchers scrambled along the bank of the dry river. A cluster of them huddled together. They strained and grunted as they heaved at a large rope, hoisting an iron cage from the canyon floor up to the edge of the platform. When the cage reached the deck, Egscar opened its gate and stepped inside. The three Crag Lurchers and Dorothy followed suit.

Egscar made a downward motion with his hand to those below and the platform commenced its irregular, creaky descent.

Dorothy gripped one bar of the swaying cage and closed her eyes, her heart rate increasing. It was a long way down. A sudden shrill cry from nearby interrupted her nervous thoughts. Dorothy shot her eyes open. As they desceneded she observed the activities inside the indentations in the canyon wall. Two youngsters wrestling. An older female stroking a younger female's hair. A group playing some sort of game with small round stones. Then Dorothy saw the source of the cry—a female Crag Lurcher cradling a restless baby. Dorothy gazed at the two of them. The mother met Dorothy's gaze with a blank stare.

The cage landed with a thud. Dorothy exhaled and let go of the bar.

Egscar opened the gate and exited.

The tall one jerked his head forward motioning for Dorothy to come. He stepped out. Dorothy and the two followed.

The Crag Lurchers who'd raised and lower the cage dropped the rope and stared, murmuring among themselves.

Up ahead, Dorothy saw the mouth of a cave in the rock face of the used-to-be waterfall. She paused.

The tall one stopped and looked back. "Come on. We're going in there."

Dorothy trudged into the cave, the chain taut from her reluctance and dread. Crag Lurchers dug and picked and hammered in the walls and floor of the cavern. Mounted torches provided light throughout the spacious cavity. The torch flames danced up and down causing the glow inside the cave to pulsate.

"What's everyone trying to find?" Dorothy said, hoping to build rapport she could exploit.

"Gold," the yellow-haired Craig Lurcher said.

"Houstess, what are you doing talking to her? You wanna get us flogged?" the red-haired one said in a lowered, demanding tone.

"Oh, come on, Harlice. She's a youngling."

Houstess calling Dorothy a youngling didn't provoke her disdain. On the contrary. His words hinted at sympathy. She could use it.

"Houstess, huh?" Dorothy said, looking at the yellow-haired one. She turned to the red-haired one. "And Harlice. My name's Dorothy. I'm from a place called Kansas."

"We wouldn't know where that is. Ever since the Nesterclop's curse, we haven't been able to travel further than the bridge," Houstess said.

Harlice shot Houstess a look. "Shut your gillyberry hole."

"Gillyberry? What's a gillyberry?" Dorothy said.

Houstess' eyes lit up. "All round-eyed Crag Lurchers LOVE gillyberries. We used to have them ALL the time before the Nesterclop's curse." He rolled his eyes to the top of his skull sockets. "Oh, how I wish I had some. I can just taste them now. Juicy and sweet with a hint of sour. Mmm." He shook his head as if a chill rushed over his body.

The tall one looked back at the three of them as he walked. "Hey! Will you stump heads knock it off already! You know what Monguzi'll do to us if you're caught talking to the prisoner."

Harlice lifted his hand. "That's what I've been trying to tell him, Nargoul, but he won't shut up."

Nargoul turned back around and continued walking.

"Monguzi?" Dorothy said.

"He's the lord of the Narrow-eyes. They rule over us Round-eyes." Houstess said.

"So, there're two kinds of Crag Lurchers, then?"

"It's been that way ever since—"

"No, Houstess," Harlice said. "Don't. It's forbidden. You've said too much already. Besides, are you blind? Can't you see what's on her face?"

Houstess wrinkled his brow and lifted an open hand. "Come on, Harlice. Look at her. Does she look like evil to you? And stop worrying. No one can hear us."

Harlice sighed.

Houstess turned his attention back to Dorothy. "Benellus used to lead us. He's the most respected of all the Round-eyes." He glanced over at Harlice. "Isn't he, Harlice?"

Harlice nodded.

Houstess continued talking as they walked deeper into the cave. "He used to be our leader. Back then all the creatures from miles around would come and drink from the river. One day, the

Nesterclop came. He pretended to be our friend. Some kind of talker he was. Monguzi and Egscar and many other Round-eyes started following him instead of Benellus. He cursed the land—gave those who followed him eyes and tongues like serpents and pointed teeth. He made them lovers of cruelty and gold. We stayed the same, but he made us slaves. He stopped the flow of the river. Put Benellus in the Prison of Keylon and made Monguzi the leader."

Nargoul turned his head to one side and spoke with a loud whisper over his shoulder, "Would you shut up! We're almost at Monguzi's lair."

Harlice cut a glance at Houstess, his teeth gritted, his brow wrinkled.

"Okay. Okay. I was just telling her how things are around here," Houstess said. "Listen, Dorothy, when we get to Monguzi's lair don't you say a word unless you're asked to speak. It could be a matter of life or death."

Dorothy nodded. "Got it,"

Egscar stopped and looked back. "Come on! Get a move on back there!"

The four of them sped up. Dorothy looked to the left and to the right as she walked. A few of the Crag Lurchers paused their work to glance at her, but most of them just toiled on without paying her any mind.

Egscar stopped at a large wooden door. He banged on it with a clenched fist. The sound reverberated throughout the cavern. A piece of wood in the middle of the door slid to one side. Two narrow eyes peered through the opening.

"We've got a special one this time," Egscar said.

The door opened. Egscar motioned with one hand for them to hurry. When they reached the doorway, he stepped inside just ahead of them. Nargoul led Dorothy in, Houstess and Harlice following close behind her.

A creature sat at a wooden table near the back wall of the lair. The leather strap stretched around his oblong skull just above his chimp-like ears securing a patch over one eye. With a scaly hand he held a nugget next to a small torch. He grinned, intoxicated with the sparkle of the yellow metal in the flickering firelight. Egscar approached the desk. "Monguzi, I have a unique one for you today."

Monguzi kept his good eye focused on the dazzling hunk of metal.

"A Round-eye found this earlier today," Monguzi said, his voice sounding as though he had a wad of phlegm lodged in his throat. He turned the nugget over in his hand and continued examining it, his eyelids thinned with delight and greed. "This is the biggest one so far. I'm sure this mountain holds many, many more in its belly. We must dig more . . . faster . . . longer. Add another five hours to the Round-eyes' workweek. Tell them—"

"The Nesterclop is sure to give you a hundred gold coins for this new prisoner," Egscar said.

Monguzi's eyes shot open wide as if he'd been hit by a surge of electricity. He raised his head slowly and looked at Egscar. "A hundred gold coins?"

"Yes sir. Just look at her," Egscar stepped aside so Monguzi could see Dorothy. He raised a hand toward her. "Isn't she something?"

Monguzi dropped the nugget on the table and rose from his chair.

"She certainly is!" he said, displaying teeth that looked like a deteriorating saw blade. "How did you acquire her?"

"Skurtz lured her to the bridge. I traded him the Hunchback's cave in exchange for her."

"The Hunchback's cave?"

Egscar's grin melted from his face. "Y-yes."

Monguzi squinted his red eye and tightened his jaw. "You gave him a hefty barter. The Hunchback's cave was our most powerful bargaining chip."

Monguzi walked from behind the desk. He worked his head from side to side causing his neck to crack.

Egscar gripped the handle of his sword with a trembling hand. "Well, considering how young she is . . . and . . . and . . . how unique she is . . . I . . . I thought that—"

"You thought, did you?" Monguzi put a crocodilian hand on Egscar's shoulder and grinned. "You made the deal of your life! I think it's time you had a lair of your own."

Egscar released his sword and smiled. "You mean it?"

Monguzi shook Egscar's shoulder then gave him a couple of firm pats. "Certainly. I'll have the Round-eyes start boring it first thing tomorrow. No more sleeping all cramped up in one of those Round-eye cubbyholes. No! You and the missus will have a roomy lair here in the mountain." He raised a gnarly finger. "Now, mind you, it won't be as big as mine."

"Oh, why of course not. You're the top Lurcher. I'm just your prodding boss," Egscar said with notable submission in tone and disposition.

Monguzzi turned and took three coins from the crooked stack on his desk. "And a fine prodding boss you are." He tumbled the coins in his hand. "As a matter of fact, I think it appropriate, given your most outstanding demonstration of shrewd trading, that you should have some gold of your very own. So here." He handed Egscar the coins.

Egscar's eyes swelled as he looked at the three coins.

A loud knock at the door interrupted the fanfare. The sentry slid the viewer open on the door and listened to the interrupter on the other side.

"All right, I'll tell him. Just a moment," the sentry said. He returned the slide to the closed position and turned to Monguzi. "Highlord, one of the taskmasters says he has an important message for you. Should I grant him access?"

Monguzi rolled his eyes. "Let him in. He knows the rule."

The sentry opened the door and the Narrow-eye walked in.

"This better be worth the intrusion," Monguzi said. "You know what I'll do if I think otherwise. To Endora you'll go."

The Narrow-eye nodded. "As these three Round-eyes were bringing the prisoner to see you." He raised a crooked finger to Houstess. "I heard this yellow-haired one tell her Crag Lurcher secrets."

Monguzi slammed both fists on the table. "What! Are you sure?"

The Narrow-eye held his confident composure. "Absolutely sure, sir. I wouldn't knock on your door if I wasn't."

Harlice wrenched his eyes shut. Dorothy glanced over at Houstess. His quivering chin and bulging eyes told of his terror. Monguzi leaned over, his boney knuckles hard pressed against the top of the table. "Is this true? Have you discussed Crag Lurcher secrets?"

Houstess looked as if someone had a knife to his throat. "Oh no, sir. Not at all. I simply told her that there are two kinds of Crag Lurchers. The stronger, wiser ones like you have narrow eyes and the weaker, more simple-minded ones like us have round eyes. That's all. You know, just so she would know how things are around here."

The reporting Narrow-eye spoke up again. "He's lying! I'm telling you he told her secret things—things that are forbidden to talk about."

Monguzi breathed in deep and exhaled. He drew down his brow and began pacing back and forth holding his chin. "Looks like we have a dilemma. Mm. Who's telling the truth?" He shot the Round-eyes a contemptuous smile. "We'll just have to find out. Won't we."

Monguzi nodded for Egscar to come close. The two of them stepped away for privacy. Monguzi put his hand on Egscar's shoulder. "We can't sell her to the Nesterclop until we're certain she knows nothing. If she says something that causes him to think we've allowed secrets to go beyond this gorge, he'll flay us both. We must take our own precautions. You know what to do, don't you?"

Egscar looked over his shoulder and leered at the Round-eyes. He turned back to Monguzi. "I know exactly what to do."

Houstess wiped the sweat from his forehead with the back of his hand. Harlice looked up at the ceiling, mouthing silent words. Nargoul looked at Houstess and shook his head, *I told you so* written on his face.

Dorothy began to say something, but Nargoul flexed an index finger over his lips to shush her. She closed her mouth.

Monguzi dropped his hand from Egscar's shoulder. Egscar turned and exited the lair.

Silence weighed heavy in the air. Dorothy felt her heart beating inside her chest. When the sentry raised the bar of the door, she jumped.

Egscar walked back in accompanied by three juvenile Crag Lurchers, budding versions of Nargoul, Houstess and Harlice.

The fathers gasped.

The three little Round-eyes trembled with watery eyes.

Monguzi turned to them, the grin of Lucifer on his face. He grabbed Nargoul's baby by the back of the neck and held it up before them. "Have you heard? Eye patches are in." He fanned his webbed fingers a few times in front of the child's face, careful to emphasize his jagged, intimidating nails.

Dorothy watched as the ghoulish leader traumatized the little one with threats of plucking its eye out. Nargoul and the others pleaded and begged for mercy.

The Round-eyes greatly out numbered the Narrow-eyes. They didn't have swords, but they did have tools. Their natures were soft and compassionate. Dorothy could use that to her advantage.

She'd show herself strong and act like a defender. Win them over. Cause a rebellion. Then she'd be out of the gorge and on her way.

Monguzi touched the baby's eyelid with his clawed thumb and index finger.

The little one cried out in horror, legs kicking.

Nargoul interlocked his fingers, fell to his knees and looked up at Monguzi. "Don't! Please!"

Monguzi paused and looked down at him. "Tell me what's been said. I'll decide if she keeps the eye."

"You're weak," Dorothy said before Nargoul could respond.

Monguzi snapped his attention to Dorothy. "What did you say?"

Dorothy gave him a despising look. "I said you're weak. All concerned about some supposed secrets getting out. You're weak. Just plain weak."

Monguzi jerked his hand up. "Silence!"

Dorothy snorted. "Or what? You gonna send me to the Endora? Is that the best you've got?"

Monguzi pulled in close to her face. "You keep talking and I'll eat you for dinner myself."

Dorothy shook her head. "Then you're just as big a fool as you are weak."

Monguzi dropped the baby Round-eye. He jerked a sword from a rack on the wall and pressed the blade to Dorothy's neck. "A foreign she-ling who chooses to run her mouth rather than avoid my stew pot. Now, that's a fool!"

Dorothy's heart pounded. She felt her blood cool in her face. "Go ahead. Take my head off. Do it! I'm not afraid to die! Are you?"

Monguzi drew the sword back in rage. "Don't think I won't!"

This was it. Her next move would end her life or expose Monguzi's role-play.

Dorothy scowled at him. "Oh please! Spare me the drama. How'd you come to be in charge here? Surely, it's not because you're the most competent. I mean, you have all the Round-eyes working day after day to mine gold for you and your stooge here." She motioned with her head toward Egscar then looked back into Monguzi's face. "He brings me to you and tells you that the Nesterclop—whoever he is—will give you a hundred gold coins for me. And you think about eating me when you could have a small fortune in gold. Really? How stupid can you be? And, on top of that, you bring these babies here and threaten to mutilate them. All over some so-called secrets. It's pathetic. Do you even HAVE a brain?"

Dorothy looked around the lair at the Crag Lurchers and raised a chained hand to Monguzi. "This . . . this is your leader? He's the best you've got. Surely, SOMEONE in this gorge has more to offer than this idiot!"

"She doesn't know what she's doing, Monguzi. She's just a child," Houstess said.

"Yes, just a child," Harlice repeated.

Nargoul stood and took a step toward Monguzi. "That's right. Just a child, Monguzi. Now please, sir, just take me. I'm the strongest Round-eye in the gorge. Take me, but let Houstess and Harlice and the younglings—"

Monguzi slammed the flat of the sword's blade on the table. "Enough. Put them in the dungeon. And take this belligerent, tar-faced she-ling too."

Whew. That bought her some time. She couldn't believe he hadn't taken her head off.

The little Round-eyes began to cry.

"Get them out of here . . . now!" Monguzi's voice echoed off the walls.

The Narrow-eyes led them out the door and back through the throat of the cavern. The daylight needled into Dorothy's eyes when she stepped out of the mouth of the cave. She stared at the ground until her pupils adjusted. The Narrow-eyes marched Dorothy and the Round-eyes along the edge of the dry riverbed. They came to a large gate of iron bars.

"Raise it!" Egscar said.

A muscular Narrow-eye stood next to a large, wooden sprocket. A leather loincloth girded him about the waist. Bronze greaves covered his shins from the bottom of his knees to the top of his leather sandals.

He grabbed one of the pegs of the sprocket and heaved it a half-turn. The taught chain from the sprocket eeked the gate up just over a foot and stopped. The Narrow-eye reached for another peg and grunted again. Once again, the bars rose the same distance. He repeated his routine until the mouth of the dungeon gapped open.

"Okay," Egscar said. "Inside."

Chapter Eight

The inside of the dungeon seemed like a giant, dry skull. Cracks like veins and sutures from ground to ceiling. Egscar shot his tongue towards the back wall to snatch a scurrying chipmunk, but the chipmunk proved to be the swifter and bolted inside a crevice near the floor. Egscar clenched a fist and grit his teeth in disappointment. "Aw! He would've been so tasty." He looked at his minions. "Let's leave these traitors to wonder what'll happen to them in the morning. This place smells like a Molewiggin latrine." He peered at Dorothy through bloodshot, snake-like eyes. "I hope you like the feel of iron because it's staying on you." Egscar bellowed a fiendish laugh then walked away. The other Narrow-eyes filed out behind him.

Like a fiendish pirate at the wheel of a death ship, the gatekeeper stood at the wooden sprocket near the mouth of the rudimentary prison. He strained as he toiled peg after peg, his defined muscles flexing as he worked. The chain screeched as it rolled off the sprocket, lowering the jagged iron bars like a dragon closing its mouth. Dorothy sat down on the bare stone floor next to Nargoul and his first-born. She hoped her theatrics back at Monguzi's lair earned her some favor with the Round-eyes. She needed their help. Their little ones were cute, she had to admit. Little versions of their fathers.

Dorothy leaned over to Nargoul and spoke in a tone just above a whisper. "I say we put our heads together and figure out how to break out of here."

Before he could respond, the gatekeeper spoke up. "No way to break out. Besides, you don't have to. I COULD release you."

Dorothy threw him a look. How could he have heard her? And why would he release them?

Nargoul waved him off. "Don't listen to him. He can't be trusted. Turned on his own brother."

"His name's Zimboza," Harlice said. "He's Benellus' brother." He rolled his eyes to the top of his head. "Or, at least he used to be."

Dorothy turned to Houstess and Harlice. "What do you mean 'used to be?'"

Harlice sneered at Zimboza. "Why don't YOU tell her?"

"Twist the story and we'll straighten it out for her," Houstess said.

Zimboza stepped from his station at the sprocket and stood in front of the prison bars. "I am the brother of Benellus. My eyes are narrow now, but we still share the same blood. To my great shame, I sided with him and rebelled against Benellus. I never imagined that the Nesterclop would banish him to the Prison of Keylon."

Nargoul looked up at Zimboza. "Why would you release us? You've never released anyone without Egscar's command?"

"Because of her." Zimboza said, pointing to Dorothy. "She has the power to break the curse. If she's willing, that is."

The Crag Lurchers turned and looked at Dorothy, Houstess and Harlice's mouths gaping open, Nargoul's brow wrinkled.

Dorothy raised one eyebrow and jerked her head back. "Me? For real?"

"Why didn't you tell us?" Houstess said.

"She didn't tell you because she's unaware," Zimboza said before Dorothy could respond. "But she's the one who can do it. This I assure you."

Nargoul's firstborn looked up at him. "Is it true, Papa? Can she really break the curse?"

Nargoul clambered for an answer. "Well . . . I . . . ah . . ."

"There," Zimboza said and pointed to the back of the dungeon. "That brown stone there. Dislodge it and you will see."

Nargoul stood and walked to over to the stone. He worked it free. In the back of the hole where the stone had been was a parchment. He reached in and took it.

"It was written by Endora's hand," Zimboza said.

"Well, what does it say?" Harlice asked.

Nargoul unfolded it and began.

A truly bad one will come. But such a one will cause change and be changed if the following be accomplished:

1. *Restore a stolen possession to its rightful master*

2. *Show tenderness to one counted unlovely*

3. *Repent of an offense in the presence of the offended*

Assistance can only be sought in one of the three. When the bad one succeeds, the curse of the Nesterclop will be no more.

Houstess released himself from his offspring's embrace. He stood up and walked over to bars of the dungeon. "Are you telling us that Dorothy is the bad one?"

Zimboza nodded. "The Devils' Spit on her face bears witness to her evil heart."

The voices of the Crag Lurchers subsided into background noise as Dorothy faded into her own contemplation about this new knowledge she'd just acquired. The revelation that she was the "truly bad one" didn't altogether repulse her. On the contrary, she welcomed it. She'd discovered bad to be an expedient character trait. It made things happen. Got things done. Mind you, she'd had some setbacks to her plans. Trusting Skurtz was a major miscalculation. It cost her the Gem-fairy's ring and her freedom as well. These, however, were but temporary postponements. Dorothy was still growing into her new, dark soul. Still learning how to utilize her new mantra—*Me first whatever the cost.* And the surfacing of this oracle . . . well, she found it to be quite appealing.

For the first time in her life Dorothy felt she possessed power. Not all that she wanted. Of course not. However, she savored the stardom she now held in the eyes of these strange beings. She sensed their sudden dependence on her. They'd rally behind her. Do whatever she asked. Give her whatever she wanted. She had no intentions of hanging around long enough to break the curse, but she'd play along with the whole "curse-breaker, liberator" thing until she achieved all she was out for. Get Toto back. Get the ring back. Get to the Emerald City. Rule and enjoy all the perks that came with it.

Dorothy's comprehension resurfaced into the Crag Lurcher's conversation as Zimboza made his final persuasive comments.

"The stain is upon her mouth. It would not be there if her heart were good and giving. She's indeed the one," he said.

Dorothy stood up. "That boy! I thought he made me play the game by the lake just so he could shame and humiliate me!"

Zimboza stuck his hands through the bars and leaned forward, reclining on his wrists. "No. He did it so that I could recognize you."

Houstess snapped his fingers. "I knew she was something special as soon as we met her."

Harlice perked up. "Me too."

Houstess gave him a frown and huffed.

Harlice shrugged his shoulders and turned his palms up. "Alright. I'll admit I was a little skeptical at first."

"Look!" one of the younglings said, pointing to the gate of dungeon.

"The Guardian Owl of Oz," Nargoul said.

The white owl perched just outside the bars. A dogwood twig with a blossom lay close to his talons. A small scroll was wrapped around the twig. The owl pushed it close to the bars. Nargoul retrieved the twig, slid off the scroll and started reading.

For the Narrow-eyes, a sleep I will make.

But when the last petal falls,

They shall most certainly awake.

The owl captivated Dorothy and the Crag Lurchers' attention, its magnificent eyes the color of a pure ocean. The noble bird made a long blink then flew away.

Zimboza pointed to Dorothy. "The Guardian's confirmed it. You're the one. Will you accept the mission?"

The Round-eyes turned their attention to Dorothy and looked at her as though they were starving and she alone could feed them.

"Your fame and legend will spread throughout all the land," Houstess said.

Dorothy scanned their faces. They were depending on her—*her*. She'd never mattered that much before. "Restore a stolen possession to its rightful master, huh?" she said.

Nargoul held up the parchment. "That's what it says."

Dorothy's stoic facial expression slowly gave way to a tight smile. "Stealing from a thief sounds like serving justice if you ask me. Any suggestions on how I might get started?"

The Round-eyes exchanged looks, each thinking the same thing but hesitant to speak. Finally, Houstess spoke up. "It's too big a task."

"Yes, it's most assuredly out of the question. Far too hazardous," Harlice said.

Nargoul pressed his lips tight and gave an affirming nod.

Zimboza leaned in close to the iron bars. "Yes, the risk is great but it must be done."

Nargoul peered at Zimboza for a moment then looked at Houstess and Harlice. He took a deep breath then exhaled and focused on Dorothy. "Okay. When we were on the bridge, Skurtz traded you to Egscar in exchange for the cave of Rantoul Grove. Remember?"

"I remember."

"The cave once belonged to the Hunchback. He was the water sentinel for all the land of the Red Brick Road. Egscar and his army stole the cave from him. Until he possesses the cave again, the land will remain dry."

"Alright. I have a score to settle with Skurtz anyway. It'll be my pleasure to take the cave from him." She lifted her hands toward Zimboza. "Get these chains off me and tell me the way."

Dorothy started toward the entrance of the dungeon. Houstess stepped in front of her, an opened hand raised. "It's not that simple. First, you'll have to FREE the Hunchback."

Dorothy shrugged her shoulders. "Okay, then I'll free him. Besides, I could use this Hunchback's help dealing with Skurtz."

Harlice walked up to Dorothy, his eyebrows peaked, his mouth half opened. "That means you'll have to travel deep inside the Darckbaal Mountain where the Molewiggins are."

"They turned the Hunchback into their hammer-swinger," Houstess said.

Dorothy felt as though a great scale hung inside her inner being. Stacked on one side of it were questions and fears. The hazards of such a quest. The unknowns. What would Darckbaal Mountain be like? The sheer name alone was mysterious and foreboding. And Molewiggins? How grotesque and dangerous could they be? Equal to the Narrow-eyes? Worse? What if they captured her? Would they kill her? What if, instead of killing her, they just held her as their life-long slave? And if they did keep her as their slave, what would they have her do? Dorothy didn't want to go there in her mind.

Piled up on the other side of the scale was her love for Toto and the possibility of getting him back. As well as the other things Dorothy craved . . . lusted for. Revenge—against Skurtz . . . against the boy. Wealth. Power. Prestige. And all the privileges that would accompany them once she ruled the Emerald City.

First, however, Dorothy would have to regain the Gem-fairy's ring. Which meant she'd have to deal with Skurtz. No small matter. Evidently, he had some kind of special powers. Like a magician he'd produced a platter of food and a jar of water. Dorothy needed backup and the Hunchback sounded like just the one for the job.

"Well, I guess I'll have to go to the Darckbaal Mountain then," she said.

Houstess looked at the other Crag Lurchers. "I think one of us should go with her. What do you think?"

Harlice reached down and picked up three pebbles from the prison floor. "I agree. Here, we'll toss to the wall to see who."

"I disagree with both of you," Nargoul said. "I don't believe any one of us should go. I say we all go."

Houstess and Harlice glared at each other. They grinned and exchanged hammered fists.

Zimboza nodded. "Very well." He looked to the back of the dungeon. "Linmar, come here."

The chipmunk scurried out from a crack in the wall and took his position standing on his back legs near the gate. Zimboza looked down at the little creature. "Retrieve the keys from Egscar."

Dorothy watched as Linmar darted through the bars and out of sight.

A chipmunk that comes when you call him and takes orders, she thought. That's amazing.

Zimboza turned his attention to Nargoul. "You should go by the Tree of Pulaski Basin. Tell the Queen of your quest. She'll give you some of her honey. It'll prove helpful when you get to Darckbaal."

Dorothy wrinkled her forehead and drew down her brow. "Honey? What do we need honey for?"

"Molewiggins love honey. They'll do anything for it," Houstess said.

"The Tree of Pulaski Basin is the only tree in all the land of the Red Brick Road where honey can still be found," Harlice said.

Linmar returned to Zimboza, Egscar's keys between his tiny teeth. Zimboza stooped down and held out a hand close to the ground. Linmar dropped the keys in it. Zimboza reached through the bars and tossed them to Nargoul. "You should get going. The younglings should remain here with me. They'll be safe behind these bars should the other Narrow-eyes awake."

Nargoul began unlocking Dorothy's shackles as Zimboza reached for a peg of the spool and heaved. The iron gate creaked upward. Nargoul, Houstess and Harlice embraced their younglings and bid goodbye.

"To Darckbaal Mountain," Nargoul said.

Houstess and Harlice looked at each other and nodded. "To Darckbaal Mountain," they said in unison.

Dorothy and the Round-eyes walked under the gate. Zimboza reached down again and Linmar climbed into his palm. He extended Linmar to Dorothy. "Here, put him in your pocket. You'll find him quite resourceful."

Dorothy took Linmar and stroked him between the ears with the end of an index finger. Linmar shut his eyes, enjoying her touch. Dorothy eased him in her pocket. She and the Crag Lurchers sat out on their journey, hiking along the edge of the dry riverbed, Narrow-eyes sleeping all around.

Chapter Nine

As Dorothy and the Round-eyes traveled further away from the gorge, the trees thinned and the high walls of the canyon declined to riverbanks.

A lime-green and maroon colored giraffe-like animal looked as though it had three beach balls lodged in its throat. It grazed among the trees and paid no attention to Dorothy and the Crag Lurchers even though they passed by within a few yards. Dorothy saw other other odd animals as well. Black and orange zebra-patterned jackrabbits. Yellow two-headed squirrels. A large green bird with a beak like a platypus. Bighorn sheep that walked on their hind legs and had hands like monkeys. A giant red tortoise that had blue wings with white polka dots. With the exception of the giraffe, every animal fled in frantic haste as soon as it made eye contact with Dorothy.

"Are the creatures around here always so skittish and fearful?" she said.

Houstess looked up at her. "It's your face that frightens them." He made a motion in front of his face as if he were drawing a circle around his mouth. "Devil's Spit sticks only to that which is evil. Gem-fairies mark the dwellings of Scaithes with it. The animals think Scaithes live inside your mouth."

The black marking on Dorothy's face terrified the animals. Not her long hair. Nothing Skurtz had told her was true.

"I'd trust a Molewiggin any day before I'd trust a Scaithe," Harlice said. "If I could get my hands on the Sword of Jerubaal, I'd slit every Scaithe from throat to gigsby." He made an aggressive slice in the air as if brandishing a sword.

"The Nesterclop brought them to our land," Nargoul said. "They're treacherous and sinister. They have the ability to deceive all that are good."

Dorothy reflected on her experience with Skurtz. He proved to be what Nargoul said—treacherous and sinister. She'd fallen victim to his trickery. Did that mean she still had some good in her? Despite what she'd done thus far? Could she go back to what she was before she started her downward descent?

"You mentioned a sword. The Sword of Jerubaal. What were you talking about?"

"It's the only weapon that can kill a Scaithe," Harlice said. "I've never seen it. But I hear that it glows like the Omnicron Star in the midnight sky. Said to be made of metal that cannot be dulled."

"Made of metal from another world," Nargoul said. "At least that's what my grandfather said his grandfather told him."

"Where is it?"

Houstess opened his mouth to reply.

"No one knows," Harlice said. "It's the stuff of mystery."

Houstess huffed and shoved Harlice on the shoulder. "Oh, come on, Harlice! I was telling the story!"

Harlice looked up at Dorothy and smiled and winked.

"Anyway, Dorothy," Houstess said. "According to legend, one must have a noble heart to wield it. It will not submit to a defrauder." Nargoul picked up his pace and moved ahead of them. "Come on," he said. "This folklore talk is slowing us down. Save your energy for walking. We can be at the Tree of Pulaski Basin by high sun if we try."

The four of them continued along the bank of the dry riverbed, Nargoul leading the way. From time to time Dorothy looked into her pocket and patted Linmar's head with the tip of her finger. The landscape of spare trees gave way to grassland and the wide dry riverbed tapered to a dry creek.

Nargoul pointed into the distance. "There."

Dorothy looked and saw the massive tree that stood alone in the midst of a sea of tall, dry grass. Linmar stuck his head out of her dress pocket.

"Linmar, we're almost there," Dorothy said.

She offered an open palm. The chipmunk obliged her invitation. He crawled up her arm and took an alert position on her shoulder as she and her new friends continued their trek.

The green sun continued to climb toward its zenith.

Dorothy wiped sweat from her forehead. "I'm awful thirsty. How might we get some water?"

"If the queen takes kindly to us, perhaps she'll give us some," Nargoul said.

"What's she the queen of?"

"All the honeybees. She used to provide honey for the entire land. But not since she moved her swarm here."

"So how do you and everyone else get honey now?"

"We don't," said Harlice. "We gather whatever nuts or berries or fruit we can find. But mostly, we have to dig for roots and leaks."

Houstess shook his head and tightened his lips. "None of our younglings have ever known the pleasure of eating honey."

"I noticed that Egscar eats dragonflies," Dorothy said. "He even tried to eat Linmar."

"That's because of the curse," Harlice said. "He used to not eat such things. None of the Narrow-eyes did when their eyes were round."

"Oh, you should have seen the land before the curse, Dorothy," Houstess said. "Everywhere you traveled on the Red Brick Road, you saw beauty and encountered kindness." He fanned his arms toward the sky. "The land of the Red Brick Road was lovely from mountain to dale. And everyone you met was your neighbor."

Nargoul stopped and turned to them. "Okay, when the queen comes out to meet us . . . if she comes out to meet us, let me do the talking. I understand she can be quite testy at times."

The great tree climbed high into the midday sky. Four colossal, half-exposed roots reached out several feet from its base then bore into the ground. A great shade encircled the ground around it as its dense foliage shielded the rays of the green sun. Dorothy and the Round-eyes approached the trunk of the mammoth living wood, its roots higher than Dorothy's head. She looked up into the leafy boughs. "Wow. I've never seen such a tree in all my life. How do you suppose we get the queen to come out?"

"I'm not sure. I guess we could try knocking. Do you see a rock laying around here?" Nargoul said.

"Here's one over here." Harlice walked over to pick it up.

He tossed the stone. Nargoul caught it with one hand. He took a deep breath and exhaled. "Okay. Let's see what happens."

Bam. Bam. Bam. Nargoul rapped on the side of the tree. He looked at Houstess and Harlice.

"Try again. This time harder," Houstess said.

Bam. Bam. Bam.

"Let's think. What else could we try?" Dorothy said.

Linmar squeaked. He scampered down her arm and hopped to the ground. Without hesitation, he scuttled to the base of the tree and into a knothole in one of the roots. Dorothy found herself becoming rather fond of the uniquely clever animal. He couldn't take the place of Toto. No other creature could, but Linmar was starting to etch out his own mark on Dorothy's heart.

Would she ever see Toto again? She'd give anything to have him back.

Linmar popped from the hole and stood erect on his two hind legs. A bee, the size of a sparrow, flew out and hovered over the tree root, studying Dorothy and the Round-eyes. It made two circuits around them then lingered close to each of their faces. And, just like that, it flew back into the knothole.

Dorothy turned to the Crag Lurchers. "Was that the queen?"

Nargoul shook his head. "No, the queen's much bigger," he said. "That was just a worker. I'd guess it flew out to see who we are and returned to report us to the queen. She and Benellus were great friends. I hope the worker recognized our round eyes."

The sound of loud buzzing came from high in the branches. Dorothy and the three Crag Lurchers stared upward. The queen emerged from a cluster of flowers and started her slow, calculated descent from the top of the giant tree. Dorothy felt the reverberation in her chest get stronger the closer the royal bee came to them. Keeping a safe distance, the queen rested on one of the main boughs where the trunk forked into the greenery. "What brings the kin of Benellus here?" she said.

"We're on a quest and need honey," Nargoul said.

"I no longer give honey to Round-eyes or anyone else. Flowers are so rare that it's all we can do to make enough to sustain ourselves. Who's this stranger that accompanies you?"

"She's the one who can break the Nesterclop's curse."

"What makes you think she can be trusted? You see the Devil's Spit on her face."

Nargoul looked at Dorothy and then back up to the queen. "There's a prophecy that one would come who's bad, but would break the curse and in so doing would become good. The marking on her face is a sign that she's the one."

The queen took flight from the bough and descended. She hovered in front of Dorothy and studied her face. The regal bee's large eyes dazzled with a plethora of colors. Her shimmering black, furry legs accented her yellowish orange torso. She moved over and lingered before Nargoul. "I'm aware of the prophecy. I've no doubt the stranger's evil. The Devil's Spit bears witness. But I'm not convinced that she's the one who can break the curse. I'll not grant your request." She started her ascent back up into the top of the tree.

Dorothy sighed. Freeing the Hunchback would be even harder now. Houstess and Harlice rounded their shoulders and looked at the ground.

Nargoul looked up in time to see the queen before she disappeared into the thick blossoms. "The Guardian Owl is helping her!"

The queen hesitated then rotated in midair. She leaned forward and flew back down to Nargoul. "The Guardian Owl is helping her?"

"Yes, and so is Zimboza," Houstess said.

Nargoul elbowed Houstess in the side.

"I see," said the queen. "And why do you request honey of me?"

Nargoul gathered his composure and squared his shoulders. "We need honey to distract the Molewiggins long enough for her to free the Hunchback. She intends to restore the cave of Rantoul Grove back to him so that he can water the land again."

The queen paused then flew back up into the heavy foliage. Dorothy and the Crag Lurchers stared up into the greenery. Suddenly, an amplified buzzing sound came from up in the tree. The queen and five other bees, about half her size, came down from the branches. Three of them clutched leaf satchels they carried by twisted vine handles. The other two held two twigs apiece. Each twig had a cluster of wax at one end that was soaked with honey and resembled a sizable lollypop.

"I hope this will be sufficient," the queen said. "I'd gladly give you more, but the flower field gets smaller and smaller with the passing of each two-moon season. The three large ones are for you to use with the Molewiggins. The four honey sticks are for your refreshment. We're counting on your success."

The three with the leaf satchels flew down and presented them to Nargoul, Houstess and Harlice. The other two gave them the honey sticks.

Nargoul looked at his honey stick and shook his head. "I thought I'd never taste honey again."

Houstess and Harlice gazed at their treats as if in a state of ecstasy, licking their lips in anticipation. Dorothy turned hers around in her hand, her stomaching rumbling in hunger. The three Round-eyes looked at each other and grinned.

Nargoul held up his honey stick. "To the good old days."

Houstess raised his. "May they soon return."

Harlice followed suit. "I second that."

With a loud buzz, the queen ascended back up into the leafy canopy, her helpers buzzing close behind her. Dorothy and the Round-eyes scarfed down their honey treats.

"Let's go. We've got a Hunchback to free," Nargoul said, an air of victory in his voice. He set out with a confident stride, a leaf satchel of honey in one hand. Houstess and Harlice traipsed along behind him, carrying theirs as well. Dorothy walked with them, listening as Houstess and Harlice reminisced about life at the gorge when the river flowed and the flowers bloomed, Linmar shifted uneasily in her pocket.

Chapter Ten

The rays of the green sun beat down on Dorothy and the Round-eyes as they hiked further from the Tree of Pulaski Basin. The flat grassland transitioned into rocky barren landscape. They topped a long hill and came to an overlook. An expansive valley of short pale vegetation spread to the right and to the left. In the distance the pastureland ended abruptly as if it had been commanded to do so by the thick forest that emerged. Beyond the woods, a skyline of mountains punctuated the distant horizon. Like a wizard's hat, one dark peak reached into the pale green sky and towered above the others.

Nargoul stopped. He brought an opened hand to his brow for shade and gazed into the distance. "There it is. Darckbaal Mountain."

"How long will it take us to get there?" Houstess said.

"Two days if we stick to the road. One if we cut through the Pontotoc Forest."

Harlice's eyes widened. "The Pontotoc Forest! Are you kidding? That's just asking for trouble."

"What kind of trouble?" Dorothy said.

"Pontotoc Forest is owned by Gnomes," Harlice said. "The archenemies of all Crag Lurchers."

"What caused such a division?"

"No one knows for sure," Harlice said. "The details have faded with time. But the breach remains."

Dorothy thought for a moment then stepped up next to Nargoul. "We should take our chances and cut through the forest. It'll save us time."

Nargoul continued gazing toward the mountain range.

Houstess made a backhanded wave. "Nargoul, I want nothing to do with Gnomes."

"Same goes for me," Harlice said. "They say they'll rob you just as soon as look at you. I don't ever want to see a Gnome." He fanned his hands.

Dorothy looked back at the two of them. "Who's they?"

Houstess and Harlice exchanged looks. Houstess shrugged his shoulders.

Harlice scratched the crown of his head. "Well, you know . . . they . . . everybody."

Dorothy turned and took a few steps toward them. "Sounds like your land is a lot like Kansas. When people back home pick up on a rumor about somebody, the tale always seems to involve 'they say.' But no one can ever tell you who 'they' are. Sometimes the truth turns out to be a lot different than what 'they' say."

Houstess bumped Harlice on the shoulder with the back of his hand. "She could be right, you know."

Harlice shook his head. "I don't think we should take any chances."

Nargoul looked back at them. "It's Dorothy's mission. Her decision. It'll be dark soon. We'll camp in the valley for the night. At first light we'll start for Pontotoc Forest. Let's get going."

Finally, they were listening to Dorothy. If it wasn't for her, the Round-eyes would still be in the gorge. Taking orders from the Narrow-eyes. Picking and digging for long hours. Getting lashed for moving too slow.

. . . .

Pontotoc Forest separated the moor from the mountain range like a sea of giant soldiers protecting a castle. Its trees grew close together as if they had been planted as a barrier to hinder any who might aim at reaching the base of the lofty heights. Dorothy and the Crag Lurchers began weaving their way through.

Dorothy squeezed between two trunks. "I've never seen such a thick forest."

Nargoul climbed over a large root. "These are the greatest and oldest trees in all our land."

Harlice followed behind Nargoul, matching his every step. "And the source of some spooky legends," he said. "I really wish we'd taken the road."

"One legend says that years ago, an army of one-eyed trolls came to Pontotoc Forest," Houstess said. "They planned to chop down some of the trees. When they drew back their axes, the tree limbs turned into giant serpents and swallowed them up."

Harlice paused and raised a trembling hand, his eyes bulging. "Another one says that the roots of these trees come alive after the sun goes down. It's said they wrap around any and all outsiders and pull them under the ground." He made a fist and jerked it downward. "And feeds them to giant hydra earthworms." He shivered and resumed walking.

A cougar screamed in the distance. Nargoul didn't flinch, but Houstess and Harlice jumped.

Harlice grabbed Houstess' arm. "Can't get me out of these woods soon enough."

"Same goes for me," Houstess said.

Dorothy rubbed her palms on her sleeves. Maybe she was wrong. Maybe they should've taken the road after all.

The trees of the legendary forest seemed to whisper with breezy voices to each other as Dorothy and the Round-eyes hiked through them. Almost with each step, Houstess and Harlice looked up into the boughs of the great trees, their faces wrenched with trepidation.

"I see daylight ahead," Nargoul said. "Must mean the forest is thinning out."

"I sure hope so," Halice said.

Houstess wiped his forehead. "I'll double that."

Beams from the sun pierced through the foliage like spotlights. Dorothy squinted as her eyes adjusted, the decrease in trees making the trek easier.

Harlice pointed. "Hey! Look! Gem-fairies must have left some water for us."

He broke into a run. The others trotted after him, Linmar looking out from the top of Dorothy's pocket.

The large vase sat at the base of a tree. Harlice picked it up to take a drink. He looked at Houstess just before he touched the rim of the jug to his lips. Houstess pulled down his brow and cut his eyes toward Dorothy.

Harlice lowered the container and smiled. "Here, Dorothy, you drink first."

She took the vase and gulped down the cold water. She poured some into a cupped hand and raised it up to Linmar's mouth before passing the jug back to Harlice. The Crag Lurchers took turns drinking, Nargoul finishing it off.

Houstess tightened this throat and pulled his chin in close to his chest. He opened his mouth and forced out the air from his stomach. "*Awwrrkk.*" He looked around. Smiled then laughed. Harlice joined in. As did Dorothy. Nargoul looked and rolled his eyes.

A force from above slammed them to the ground. The impact knocked the honey baskets out of the Crag Lurchers' hands. Before they could get up, something scooped them off their feet. Dorothy's stomach swooped. Her feet tangled in what looked like the ropes of a net beneath her.

Dorothy and the Round-eyes hung suspended above the forest floor, honey dripping.

A tall, ghoulish figure stepped from behind a tree and strolled toward the net. "Well, well, well. What do we have here?"

Dorothy and the Crag Lurchers strained and wrestled against the net to gain an upright position.

"I count four of them. They'll make for a nice payday. The Nesterclop will pay us a tidy sum for this catch. Don't you think, Razorlick?" came a deeper voice from the opposite direction.

Dorothy peered through the net. "Scaithes!"

"I didn't know they lived this far from the gorge," Houstess said.

"I knew we should've taken the road," Harlice said.

The second Scaithe came near the net. He poked a gnarly finger inside and raked Dorothy's hair. "Now, this one's unique." He pressed his hideous face against the net. "Oh! Look at the Devil's Spit on her face. We may have a lot in common."

Razorlick snapped his fingers. "Let them down and tie their hands."

Three other Scaithes emerged from behind the trees. Two of them lowered the net to the ground and the other spread the noose of it open. Dorothy's heart pounded as she prepared to run.

Razorlick curled one side of his mouth. "Try to run and I'll feed you to the crocs at Hex Lagoon."

The Scaithes yanked and shoved Dorothy and the Round-eyes as they tied their hands behind their backs. Razorlick jerked his head, motioning the command to follow him.

Dorothy caught a glimpse of something white up in the trees. She cut a look. The Guardian Owl.

Chapter Eleven

Razorlick and his eerie clan led Dorothy and the Round-eyes farther into the Pontotoc Forest until they came to a tree, its girth as big as a windmill head. On one side of the tree's gargantuan trunk massive roots curved and drilled downward forming an arbor. A plethora of smeared black covered the roots and reached over the peak of the arch. Devil's Spit.

"Stake them," Razorlick said.

Nargoul's escort thrust a firm hand to the side of his shoulder. Nargoul stumbled at the impact. The escort pointed to a barren section on the forest floor. "Sit!"

The other Scaithes handled Dorothy, Harlice and Houstess in like fashion.

Rusty iron stakes stuck out of the hard dirt. The Scaithes tied the four of them to the stakes and looked to Razorlick for further instruction.

"Let's eat before we take'm to the Nesterclop," he said.

Razorlick walked under the arch of the tree's roots. He climbed down the ladder that leaned against the top of a hole in the ground under the trunk. The other Scaithes followed suit, muttering as they went. Dorothy and the Crag Lurchers sat in silence, listening to make sure all their captors were down in the cavern.

Houstess turned to Nargoul. "Any ideas?"

Nargoul started twisting and pulling at the rope that bound him. "I'm trying to get . . . loose from . . . this stake."

Harlice shut his eyes and shook his head "It's no use. It's the Nesterclop for us."

Linmar crawled out of Dorothy's dress pocket and onto the ground. He scurried behind her and began gnawing away at the rope that bound her hands.

Dorothy smiled and raised her eyebrows. "Hey, Linmar's chewing at the rope." She twisted her chin just over her shoulder. "That's it, Linmar. That's it."

The sound of voices came from the tree as two Scaithes began climbing the ladder. "Let's see what they look like," one said to the other.

The Scaithes exited through the arch and came close.

"Well, Gutso. It seems we have three Crag Lurchers."

Gutso sighed. "Craig Luchers. Useless and worthless." He raked his ghastly fingernails through Dorothy's hair. "But, this one. Now, this one looks promising."

Dorothy pulled her head away. Gutso grabbed her by the chin to inspect her face. "Her face, Linktoo. It's been marked."

Dorothy raised one side of her lip and jerked away from his grip.

Linktoo displayed his uneven gray and yellow fangs. "She has spunk too."

A rustling in a nearby bush peaked the two Scaithes' attention. They looked at each other, their grins exposing their barbed teeth.

"Are you thinking what I'm thinking?" Linktoo said.

Gutso licked his teeth with his forked tongue. "I'm thinking a hare."

They bolted to the bush and began rummaging through its foliage.

Careful not to bite into Dorothy's tender flesh, Linmar severed the last fiber of the rope.

"I'm loose," Dorothy said.

Nargoul turned to her. "Then go."

"But they'll—"

"Nargoul's right," Houstess said. "Go while you have the chance."

"The hope of the land rest with you," Nargoul said. "Not us. Now go."

"It'll only take me a second to untie you and we can all go together."

"We can't afford to take that chance. Now go before they see you."

Dorothy hesitated.

Harlice raised his brow. "Run, Dorothy. While you have the chance."

Dorothy pushed the cut rope from her hands. "Let's go, Linmar."

The chipmunk sprang to the lap of her dress and back into her pocket. Dorothy eased herself up, careful not to make a noise. She slipped behind a tree. Then sprinted away into the forest.

· ·

Dorothy propped against a towering evergreen. She scanned the forest, her chest expanding and contracting as she breathed in and out. Waiting to recover so that she might sprint again.

What would happen to Nargoul, Houstess and Harlice. They'd sacrificed their chance at freedom to ensure hers. She owed them her life. A needle of shame pricked her conscience. Would she have done the same for them?

A flapping commotion in the treetops interrupted her contemplation. She looked up in the direction of the sound. The Guardian Owl sat perched on a limb, his piercing eyes fixed into hers. The bird flew down and rested on a low bough not far from Dorothy's reach. It took a slow, deliberate blink then lifted up from the tree and flew the distance of a stone's throw. Hovering in midair, it turned back to look at Dorothy. It made a screeching sound. Flew a little further. Hovered again and looked at her once more.

Dorothy wiped her forehead with her the back of her hand. Did it want her to follow it? Okay, if that was what it wanted.

Dorothy ran, following the owl's lead. It would fly a short distance, perch and wait for her, then, resume flight when she drew close. The owl repeated the routine again and again, leading Dorothy further and further into the Pontotoc Forest.

Finally, it landed on a large stone. When Dorothy approached, the creature ascended through the treetops and flew away.

Dorothy studied her surroundings. Trees in every direction. A sparse growth of ferns. No signs of wildlife. Just beyond the large stone a bush sprawled over the ground, its green foliage dotted with small purple fruit.

Okay. The berries. The owl had led her there for the berries. She was hungry, she had to admit. She strolled over to the bush and picked a few. Mm. Delicious. As she chewed she plucked another handful and crammed them into her mouth.

"And jes who tole you that you could help yerself to our gillyberries?" a brash voice said from behind her.

Dorothy spun around to see a knee-high sized man dawning a pointed leather hat. At the sight of Dorothy's face, the man's eyes shot open wide and his chin dropped. He pulled his hat from

his head and clutched it with both hands in front of his belly. "Oh . . . I . . . I'm sorry. You jes go ahead and help yerself. Don't mind me none. I . . . I'll just be on my way." He started backing away.

Dorothy stepped toward him. "I won't hurt you."

"If it's all the same to you, I really should be going. I've got . . . uh . . . I've got an appointment. That's right. An appointment. So, I'll be seeing you."

The little man eased his hat on his head then turned and ran.

Dorothy trotted after him. "Please! Please come back!"

The man looked back over his shoulder. His foot caught on a fallen branch and he tumbled to the ground. "Ugh!" he cried out. He grabbed his ankle and held it.

Dorothy approached him. "Oh, you've hurt yourself. Let me take a look at it." She stooped down and reached out a hand to touch him.

The man raised a palm, his eyes wide open. "Now, don't you come any closer." He began scooting away from her on his backside. "If you do, I'll . . . I'll put a hex on you. You can tell yer granny that."

"I only want to help you. Please don't put a hex on me."

The man stopped and cracked a grin. "So, you do fear my hexing pow'rs after all, do ye?"

Dorothy nodded.

"Who are ye and where're ye from?"

"My name is Dorothy. I'm from a place called Kansas."

"Kansas, huh?"

"Yes, and I plan to get back there just as soon as my mission is complete."

The man shut one eye. "And jes what might yer mission be?"

"Undoing the Nesterclop's curse."

The man cocked his head and looked at Dorothy with his brow pulled down. "Sure. And I'm the Wizard of Oz."

"You're mocking me. You don't believe me. Do you?"

The dwarf gentleman picked up his hat and stood to his feet, favoring his ankle. He flopped the hat on his head and peered into Dorothy's eyes.

"You got Devil's Spit on yer face. So, I'm bettin' every word that comes out of yer mouth is a witch-tooth flimflam, a spider-egg scheme or a goozle-tongue lie. I'm keeping my eye on you because at any moment you could change yourself into a Molewiggin or Dobbledoogin."

Dorothy fanned both hands. "No. No. It's not what you think. I . . . ah . . ." She pulled her brow down and tightened her lips. "It's a long story. This black stuff on my face identified me as the one who could break the curse. How's your ankle?"

"It'll be fine. Wouldn't be surprised if it's fine already. My kind are pow'rful healers as well as potent hexers. You can tell yer granny that."

The man looked away, rubbing his chin and mumbling.

Dorothy leaned in to hear. "What's that you say?"

"Oh, I wuz just thinkin' you and I could strike a deal."

Dorothy narrowed her eyelids. "What kind of deal did you have in mind?" She was learning that deals could be costly in the land of the Red Brick Road.

"Would you believe that I've been ah wantin' to go to Kansas most of my life. Got some kin folks there."

Dorothy relaxed her expression. "You don't say. I've never met or heard of any people like you in Kansas."

The little man raised an index finger. "Oh, yes. They're there. You just have to know where to look fer'em. What's been ah hinderin' me is the fact that I have a double ticket."

"A double ticket?"

He shoved his hands into his pockets. "Yep. A ticket that's only good if two folks travel. Won't work fer jes one."

Dorothy cocked her head and looked at him with suspicion. "Why, I never heard of such a thing."

The man pulled one hand from his pocket and shook his index finger. "See, that's because you never traveled on the Tishmingo Silverbolt."

"Tishmingo Silverbolt?"

"The finest and the fastest locomotin' train to ever run a rail." The man winked. "You can tell yer granny that."

"That's funny. Since I've been in the land of the Red Brick Road no one's even mentioned it."

"Because it doesn't run in these parts. You have to go all the way to where the Whatchamagolly River feeds into the Somethingadilly Lake," he said, making a large dome motion with one hand. "There you can board the Tishmingo Silverbolt and she'll take you clean to Kansas." The little man put his thumbs under his suspenders. "So, would you like to hear my deal?"

Dorothy looked down at him. "I'm listening."

He grinned. "Both of us want to go to Kansas. Right?"

Dorothy gave a firm nod. "Right!"

"So, if you'll forget about all yer curse undoing, we can leave in say . . . ah." The man pulled a pocket watch from his trousers and looked at it. "In exactly thirteen minutes." He returned it to his pocket. "And for making the journey with me, I'll give you a fortune of gold."

He took off his hat and held it before her. Shiny gold coins filled the hat almost to the top. Dorothy gazed at the coins, her eyes bulging, her mouth open. "My word! I've never seen so much money."

The man returned the hat to his head. "I'll give you the gold when we board the train. Now, do we have a deal?"

"Can I have a moment to think about it?"

"I reckon. But make it quick. That train'll be departin' soon just as shore as breakfast is et before lunch."

Dorothy turned away from him. She folded her arms and took several steps. Leaning on one shoulder against a tree she thought of what she could do with the money back in Kansas. She could buy a fancy house in town. Or even better, build THE fanciest house in town. She'd be the youngest homeowner anyone'd ever heard of. She could have maids and cooks. Fine food. And clothes—beautiful clothes. And shoes. And jewelry. Enough to out do Molly Anne Brewster ten times over. She could pay off Aunt Em and Uncle Henry's farm—if she wanted to. She would want to, wouldn't she? Of course she would. They were the ones who'd fed her, clothed her and, most importantly, loved her. They'd sacrificed a lot for her. And speaking of sacrifice, the Round-eyes REALLY sacrificed. They'd saved her life. While she was pondering what to do with a gold fortune, they were probably well on the way to the Nesterclop. Whoever he was.

Dorothy looked down at the toes of the slippers. They seemed to transform into small mirrors on the tops of her feet. The reflections of her marred face reminded her of what she'd done. What she'd become. She wondered if the Gem-fairy princess got out of the bog. She should've saved her. Skurtz turned out to be a complete liar. He'd lied about the princess as well no doubt. He wanted the ring so he used Dorothy to get it. And she let him. All because she wanted fame, wealth and power.

Me first whatever the cost had consequences. For others. For Dorothy too. How could she ever live with herself now after what she'd done? To the princess. To the old man back at the depot. She couldn't go back and change things. What she could do, however, was forget. Forget *Me first whatever the cost,* and everything else the man had told her. And, she could start doing the things she knew to be right—the things that'd make Aunt Em and Uncle Henry proud.

Dorothy pressed her lips together. She'd made up her mind.

She stood up and spun around. "Your offer is most kind and thoughtful. I wanna go back to Kansas. Like . . . yesterday. I want money and all the beautiful things it can buy."

The little man winked, grinning. "Got an eye for that gold, do ye?"

"But my answer is no. I've got a mission to complete—an important one. And I have friends to rescue too . . . if it's not too late. I've got to free the Hunchback and I want to find my dog, Toto. I'd love for you to come along. I certainly could use your help. But you have an appointment. So, I'll be on my way. A pleasure to meet you and I'm glad your ankle feels fine. Good day."

Dorothy started walking.

"Wait! Don't go jes yet!" the man said.

Dorothy stopped and turned around "So you'll help me?"

"I ain't sayin' I will and I ain't sayin' I won't. You can't expect me to just throw in wi'ye without hearing more of the detailments."

"Certainly, Mister . . . uh."

"Clyde Erskine Sweetwater Festerburton the Third. But my friends call me Sput."

He offered her a handshake.

Dorothy obliged with a big smile. "I'm very glad to meet you, Sput."

Sput released her hand and shook his index finger at her. "You'll get gladder and gladder in the days to come. I'm a man of broad and copious experiences . . . broad and copious. You can tell yer granny that." He shoved his hands into his pockets again. "Now, I'll be ah hearin' them detailments I requested."

"Oh yes. First of all, are you afraid of Scaithes?"

Sput cocked his head to one side and looked at her from the corners of his eyes. "Scaithes, you say?"

Dorothy nodded.

"Well, I don't prefer'em. But I ain't never give into one. You can tell yer granny that." He swelled his chest and thumbed his beefy nose.

"I have three very special friends. Some Scaithes have them. I plan to free them."

"Uh huh." Sput began to pace back and forth. "Tell me about these friends."

"They're Crag Lurchers."

Sput tensed up like he'd come face to face with a ghost, his eyes wide and bulging. "Crag Lurchers! Why I'd rather have ingrowns in all ten of my toes than to help a wad ah Crag Lurchers."

"How can you say such a thing? They're about as nice as anyone you could ever know."

"Ha! They've got the sassafras leaves pulled over your eyes. I'm here to tell you they'll rob ye as soon as look atcha."

Dorothy drew down the corners of her mouth and lowered her chin. "And, you've had such a misfortune?"

Sput shook his head. "Well, not me personally. But I'm sure many ah Gnome has."

"Do you know some who've been robbed by Crag Lurchers?"

Sput hooked a clinched fist in the air. "Why you ah askin' me all these lawyerin' questions? I don't have to know a Gnome robbed of a Crag Lurcher to know such to be the truth. I've heard tell of their lowdownin' ways since I was knee high to a fiddle bug. If it's talk among Gnomes then it's pert near golden. You can tell yer granny that."

"Sounds to me that Gnomes and Crag Lurchers have at least one thing in common."

Sput folded his arms. "And jes what might that be, Kansas?"

"What if I told you I've heard that Gnomes will rob you as soon as look at you?"

"I'd say you'd heard a lie plain and flat out. We Gnomes . . ."

Dorothy called him on it before he could finish his sentence. "Oh, I see now. You're a Gnome yourself."

"Yes, and ah mighty proud of it. We Gnomes are respectable and valiant."

"And humble too," Dorothy mumbled.

"What's that you say?"

"Nothing, nothing. I was just thinking out loud. You Gnomes are respectable, are you?"

"Yes, by cracky."

"And valiant?"

Sput straightened up, his clenched his fists at his sides, his head held high. "As much as any lord in the land of Oz."

Dorothy raised her eyebrows and looked him dead in the eyes. "Then, it would seem to me that you'd jump at the opportunity to exercise your high character qualities by helping those who are in need even if they are Crag Lurchers. That is, unless you're just long on talking and short on ACTUALLY being valiant."

Sput pulled his hat from his head and walked several steps away from Dorothy, clutching the brim with both hands.

He stopped and turned around to face her. "All right then, Kansas. But if they steal any of my gold, I'll be expecting you to pay me back two to one. Deal?"

Dorothy displayed a big toothy smile. "Deal."

Sput put his hat back on his head and rubbed one side of his chin with an opened hand. "We's goin' fuedin' with Scaithes, huh?"

"Yes. They're holding my friends at a big tree not far from here. Devil's Spit's smeared all over it. It's got roots you can walk under and a big pit under it too. I think they live in it."

"That'd be Razorlick's clan. This ain't gonna be no berry pickin'. You can tell yer granny that. We're gonna need some reinforcements. Wait here."

Sput walked over to the stone the owl had led Dorothy to. "Maher-shalal-hash-baz," he said.

The flat side of the stone turned liquid-like and began to ripple. A large, sleepy face surfaced. It opened its eyes. Upon seeing Sput, it replied, "Very well," and opened its mouth. Sput stepped inside. The mouth and eyes closed and the face disappeared. The rock, once again, looked like any other ordinary boulder.

Dorothy reached into her pocket and lifted Linmar. He opened his eyes from the nap he'd been taking.

She rubbed the chipmunk between the eyes with the tip on her finger. "Hungry?"

Dorothy strolled over to the bush. She picked a gillyberry and gave it to Linmar. Her faithful pocket friend held the berry in his front paws, nibbling. Dorothy plucked more for herself and munched on them as she waited for Sput to return. In the place of each berry she took, a new berry grew in its place.

"There she is," said Sput.

Dorothy turned around. Sput stood with a finger pointed at her. The huddle of Gnomes around him gazed at Dorothy, each with a notable look of uneasiness on his face.

One pushed his spectacles up on the bridge of his nose. "Are you sure about this, Sput? Look at'er face."

"Sorry, fellers. I forgot to tell ye that she's got Devil's Spit on her face. Don't let that worry ye none though. She passed the Okie Dokie Test."

Dorothy wrinkled her brow. "What's the Okie Dokie Test?"

"Oh, you know all that I said about a double ticket to ride the Tishmingo Silverbolt to Kansas?"

"Uh huh."

"Well, it wuz all a pot full uh possum feathers. And there weren't no gold in my hat. It wuz all a shenanigan fer yer eyes."

One of the Gnomes stepped from the huddle and turned to the others. "I say we commence out on our feudin' march to Razorlick's tree!"

"Yup, we've gnawed the grease enough," Sput said. "Danworth, go down and get the Wardin' Staff!"

One of the Gnomes turned to the big rock and uttered the word, "Maher-shalal-hash-baz." The face appeared again and opened its eyes. "Very well," it responded and opened its mouth. Danworth walked inside.

"What's the Warding Staff?" Dorothy said.

"It's an ancient staff, crafted by Argorooni, the mightiest, wisest Gnome ever to live," Sput said. "Scaithes are ah feared to death of it. You can tell yer granny that."

"A vermin Scaithe knows if his neck ever gets in it, he's banished to the bottom of the Devil's Spit Spot!" one of the other Gnomes said.

Sput lifted one leg and slapped his knee. "Aw come on, Fisselborn, I was doin' the tellin'!"

"I know you wuz. I also knowd if I was ah wantin' to tell any of it, I'd have to jump in and take my place in the tellin'."

Fisselborn chuckled. The others began to laugh. Sput shook his head, an irritated look on his face.

Danworth stepped from behind the rock holding a golden staff. It had a crook at one end, the tip of which was adorned with a large, purple stone. Danworth handed the Warding Staff to Sput.

Fisselborn spoke up again. "When a Sciathe's near, the end—"

Sput jumped in before Fisselborn could finish. "The end will glow."

Sput smiled and looked at Fisselborn. "Now, we're even."

Fisselborn rolled his eyes and returned a reluctant nod.

"So very much like Round-eyes," Dorothy mumbled.

"What's that you say?" Sput asked.

"I was just thinking how we should get going while it's still daylight."

Sput turned to his fellow Gnomes and raised the Warding Staff in the air. "Okay, fellers. Let's go give Razorlick and his crudskimmers what fer!"

The Gnomes cheered and hyped themselves, marching behind Sput. Dorothy brought up the rear, Linmar on the lookout from the top of her dress pocket, the Guardian Owl gliding through the tree foliage above.

Chapter Twelve

Nargoul, Houstess and Harlice sat staked to the ground close to the giant, ghastly tree, its bottom limbs drooping down just above their heads like the fingers of a skeletal host.

"Nargoul," Houstess said. "What does the Nesterclop do with Round-eyes?"

"Trades them to the Molewiggins for slaves. If they're weak, he feeds them to the crocs at Hex Lagoon. Or worse."

Harlice swallowed a painful lump. "What could possibly be worse?"

Nargoul looked at him with a solemn expression. "He's been known to eat them himself. I heard once that a Scaithe captured a northern Round-eye and traded him to the Nesterclop. The Nesterclop strung him up. Alive! Then, ate him bit by bit. Took him seven days. One day he cut off a leg and ate it. The next day an arm. The next day—"

"I don't want to know," Harlice said. "I never wanted to come through this forest. If we'd just taken the road we'd probably be almost to Darckbaal Mountain by now."

Houstess looked up into the treetops. "Remember when we climbed to the top of Peg Leg Cliff and then were too scared to get ourselves back down? Benellus and Zimboza had to climb up and get us."

The memory melted the tense expression from Harlice's face. He smiled. "My motherly made me pick two bushsackles of gillyberries for each of them. She told me if she caught me eating even one berry she'd make it three bushsackles."

"Yeah, my popsie called me Chickity until I climbed back to the top of Peg Leg and got myself down on my own," Nargoul said.

They laughed.

"And the time it rained for three days," Harlice said. "We stole Egscar's shield and used it to sled down Froggy Bottom Hill?"

"Oh, that was a fine thrill. We thought he'd be mad when he found out. Instead, he took a go down the hill himself. I never saw him laugh so hard in all my days," Houstess said.

Nargoul turned and looked at Houstess. "Egscar was like an uncle to us before the curse. Not a nicer Crag Lurcher in all the gorge. Those were the days—honey in the spring and summer—gillyberries year-round—animals drinking from the river. Maybe Dorothy . . ." his voice drained off.

The sounds of Scaithes snatched the reflective moment. Their raspy voices grew louder as they made their ascent from the hole underneath the tree. The Crag Lurchers ceased their talking. Nargoul's winsome demeanor washed from his face. Houstess and Harlice looked at each other and swallowed hard lumps in their throats.

"No one ever had a greater friend than you, Harlice," Houstess said, his voice quaking.

"The same goes for you Houstess," Harlice said, just as emotional.

Razorlick and his minions emerged from the arch and strolled over to them, their reptilian stomachs bulging from their feasting.

Razorlick shot his eyes open and gritted his serrated teeth. "The foreigner's escaped! Where's Gusto and Linktoo?"

"Must be out searching for the foreigner," one of the Scaithes said.

"If those imbeciles let her get away, I'll throw them both to the crocs. Hopefully they have enough brains to find her and catch up with us. Untie these three. We need to get moving."

Three Scaithes jumped at the command and untied the Round-eyes.

Razorlick looked down at the three Crag Lurchers. "Stand up!"

They stood, their hands still bound behind their backs.

Razorlick walked to them and stooped down to make eye contact. His breath reeked with the smell of carrion. "Do you know where the foreigner ran off to?"

Razorlick looked into Harlice's eyes. "You know. Don't you?"

Harlice looked away.

Razorlick turned his attention to Houstess. "How about you? Got enough sense to save your hide?"

Houstess shook his head.

"I see. Brainless too, are you?"

He stepped up to Nargoul and sized him up from head to foot. "You're the brave one. Perhaps you're smart as well. You take me to her and I'll let you and your friends here go. What do you say to that?"

Nargoul peered back at him and raised one side of his lip. "Go sit on a sword."

Razorlick struck Nargoul across the jaw with the back of his hand. "Have it your way. It's the Nesterclop for the three of you."

"No, it's the Devil's Spit Spot for you! You can tell yer granny that!" Sput said and raised the Warding Staff in the air, the purple stone glowing.

Razorlick looked up. His sneer turned to an expression of horror as Sput marched toward him. The other Gnomes stepped out from the forest tree line, twirling bolas over their heads.

Razorlick and the Scaithes back stepped.

"Now listen, Gnome," Razorlick said, his hands raised. "We desire no conflict with you. Besides, we're half as many. Let us return to our den. The Crag Lurchers can go free."

"Yes," Sput said. "The Crag Lurchers will go free. But not ner one of you reprehending Scaithes'll return to yer den."

Razorlick and the Scaithes bolted in different directions.

Sput looked back at the fifty plus Gnomes. "Pull!"

The Gnomes flung their bolas. The roped stones helicoptered through the air and fettered the Scaithes at their ankles. They fell with a thud. Sput ambled over to them as they screamed and screeched. One by one, he hooked the crook of the Warding Staff around their ghastly necks. And, one by one, the grotesque bodies of each Scaithe transformed into a banshee that rose from the ground as if lapped up by a great force from high above the forest. Their cries grew fainter as the force carried them away and deposited them in the Devil's Spit Spot.

The Gnomes untied Nargoul, Houstess and Harlice. The three Round-eyes massaged the soreness out of their wrists and stretched their webbed fingers.

Houstess began shaking hands with the Gnomes. "Thanks for everything. Thought we were goners for good."

Harlice followed Houstess' lead. "I never been so scared in all my life."

Nargoul looked on stoically. What was he thinking? This was not time to withhold appreciation. With apprehension he extended his hand to Sput. "I'm Nargoul."

Sput hesitated, locked onto Nargoul's eyes. He cracked a thin smile, wiped his palm on his trousers and returned the handshake. "To those dwellin' above and below the ground I'm known as Sput."

"I never thought I say this to a Gnome," Nargoul said. "But thank you. You saved our lives. Is there anything we could do to repay you?"

Sput waved a hand toward Nargoul. "Aw, no need. We shoulda banished Razorlick and his bunch a long time ago. I guess it wuz one ah them chores that we jes never got round to doin' till Kansas showed up."

Dorothy stepped up to the two of them. "What the two of you should do is reconcile."

Nargoul raised an opened hand. "Now, listen, Dorothy—"

Sput rubbed his chin. "That fire's been a burnin' fer a powerful long time. We . . . ah . . . we'll have to do some think-a-latin' on that."

Dorothy wrinkled her brow and pointed to the two of them. "I mean it. There's no reason why the Crag Lurchers and Gnomes shouldn't bury the hatchet. Neither of you can give a single good reason for butting heads. All you know is something happened a long time ago. So long, in fact, that nobody knows what that something is." She turned to Sput. "Sput, you don't know a single Gnome that's been robbed by a Crag Lurcher, do you?"

Sput frowned and shook his head.

Dorothy leaned in closer to Nargoul's face. "And you, Nargoul. All you've been going on is some rumor that's been passed down for who knows how long."

Nargoul lowered his eyes then looked at Harlice and Houstess and shrugged his shoulders.

"You just asked if there was anything you could do to repay him, didn't you?"

Nargoul nodded. "And I mean it. If ever you need us, we'll be there. Right fellas?"

"Ab-so-lutely!" Houstess said.

Harlice grinned. "Double that for me."

Dorothy spread her hands apart. "Why not do something bigger than just returning a favor? Why not set a new direction that'll benefit others for generations to come? Whataya say?"

Nargoul and Sput peered at each other, their faces yielding to grins.

"I'll see to that every Round-eye in the canyon knows that Gnomes saved our lives," Nargoul said. "When Dorothy breaks the curse, every Gnome is invited to come to the gorge to feast and celebrate. And, I promise you—"

Sput raised a palm. "Now, hold on a minute. Let me get some speechifying in too. I want you and all Crag Lurchers to know that Pontotoc Forest is yer home away from home. We'd count it a priv-ah-lege to have you anytime. There's elbow room a plenty. Furtherwise, consider any gillyberry bush in Pontotoc Forest to be as much Crag Lurcher as it is Gnome." He jammed the end of the Wardin Staff on the ground. "Now, about this curse undoing business. If you're going to Darckbaal Mountain, you could use a few extra hands." He scanned the faces of the other Gnomes. "I say we throw in and help Dorothy and these Crag Lurchers. You agreein'?"

The Gnomes shouted with enthusiasm.

Sput turned to Dorothy. "Well, it's unanimous, Kansas. We's commencing to Darckball Mountain. You can tell yer granny that."

The new comrades set out for the ominous mountain. Sput and Nargoul led the way, exchanging stories of what they'd heard about the old days when Gnomes and Crag Lurchers lived as friends in Pontotoc Forest. With Linmar on her shoulder, Dorothy kept step, taking in the handed-down legends. Houstess, Harlice and the other Gnomes joked and carried on as they followed the leaders. The Guardian Owl kept watch from the sky above. Back at the gorge, Zimboza picked up a fallen dogwood petal. Three remained on the twig.

Chapter Thirteen

Like a giant standing in the midst of dwarfs, Darckbaal Mountain's summit rose above its neighboring peaks. Its base sprawled out like a massive tent that had been pitched downward to the tree line of the Pontotoc Forest. Foreboding, jagged ridges, as if clawed by a colossal hand from above, rose along the mountain's surface.

Dorothy and her companions emerged from the perimeter of the forest, Sput resting the Warding Staff over one shoulder as he carried it. Nargoul, Houstess and Harlice each held the bolas they'd made with the help and instruction of the Gnomes while journeying through the forest.

They drew near to the base of the mountain.

"Here we are. Darckbaal Mountain," Nargoul said.

Sput leaned the Warding Staff against a large stone. He removed his hat, pulled the handkerchief from his back pocket and wiped the sweat from his forehead. "This mountain's cloaked in mysteries and tall tales."

Harlice swallowed a hard lump. "What kind of mysteries and tall tales?"

"My grandpappy told me that, when he wuz just a young whippersnapper, his grandpappy told him this mountain was once the crown jewel of the land. All kinds of critters lived on it. All kinds of trees grew on it too. And steps went clear to the top so's ye could go up and see clear to the Emerald City."

Well, it was anything but friendly looking now.

"What happened?" Dorothy asked.

Sput pushed his hat back on his head and crammed the handkerchief back into his pocket. "Let's all catch our breath a bit and I'll tell ye."

The Gnomes and Crag Lurchers took seats on stones and on the ground.

"As legend tells it," Sput began. "A pow'rful, great-hearted king once ruled all the lands of the colored roads. He lived inside the mountain. A more just and noble ruler, one could not imagine. Each day, he'd climb the steps and survey the lands to make sure all were gettin' along and doin' fine. One day he called a special meetin'. The gov'ners of all the lands came. From the Purple Road clean to the Orange Road. He told 'em he was goin' fer away for a time in order to establish his kingdom in other lands. And, he instructed'em to take care of things while he'uz away. Told'em to exercise the same goodwill and benevolence like they'd seen in him. Things were pleasant fer a time."

Sput paused and motioned to some of the Gnomes. "We'll be ah havin' them gillyberries now. It's been a spell since breakfast."

Five Gnomes stepped forward, bulging sacks on their backs. They lowered their shoulders and eased the sacks down to the ground.

"Help yerself," Sput said with a grin and a wink. "And that goes double for you Crag Lurchers."

The Gnomes opened the sacks began passing them around.

"Things were pleasant for a time, you say," Houstess said as he chewed, one of his cheeks round with gillyberries.

Sput tossed a berry into his mouth. "Yup." He scowled and shivered. "Whew, that one wuz picked a little too early." He regained his composure and continued. "Shortly after the king departed, the governors quarreled over who would be chief among'em. They argued, protested, objected, and fussed. No agreement could be reached. And so each one went back to his land, vowing to have nothing to do with the others. Eventually, the governor of the Red Brick Road died. No one was in line to take his place. Fer years the land had no governor. Then, the Nesterclop came and he brought the Molewiggins and Scaithes with'im. He cursed the land. Gave the mountain to the Molewiggins and everything else to the Scaithes. These are the things I've heard tell of. Whether they be true altogether or just true here a little and there a little, I don't know. We Gnomes never gave mind of venturing out of the forest. That is, until you, Kansas." Sput looked at Dorothy and pointed an index finger. "And told us about yer determinizin' to undo the Nesterclop's curse."

"Whoo! Whoo!" came a sound from a tree at the edge of the forest. Dorothy turned to look. The Guardian Owl made a long blink then lifted from the limb and flew along the base of the mountain.

Dorothy rose from the stone she was sitting on. "Let's go. He's showing us the way."

Sput reached for the Warding Staff.

Dorothy and her band followed the owl as it flew close to the ground, stopping routinely and allowing them to keep up. The bird perched on a boulder next to a weathered stone stairway and waited. When Dorothy drew close it flew to a higher vantage point along the hewn steps.

She started hiking the ascent, Linmar in position on her shoulder, the others following. The Guardian Owl took flight and disappeared into the forest.

Sput took slow, deliberate steps, the Warding Staff shaking in his trembling hand. "We Gnomes are potent and resourceful low to the ground. But high up questing causes our inner constitutions to quiver."

Houstess looked back at him and reached out a hand. "Here, let me carry the Warding Staff so you can use both hands."

One of the Gnomes lost his footing and slipped over the edge. He cried out in terror as he clung to the edge of the precipice, his feet dangling.

As quick as a snap, Harlice grabbed the little man by the collar of his shirt.

The Gnome kicked as Harlice held him suspended over the side of the mountain. Harlice grunted, then lifted him up and returned him to the walkway.

The Gnome embraced Harlice. "Oh, sweet honeysuckle julep. I was a goner fer sure. Thank you. Thank you. I owe you my life."

Harlice clapped his palms on the Gnome's back as they hugged. "If it wasn't for you, it would've been the Nesterclop for me for sure."

The Gnome released him and gave a teethy smile. "Ah, so we're even then."

Harlice rested a hand on one of the Gnome's shoulders. "We're friends. Friends don't keep a tally of good deeds. They just look out for one another because they love . . . I mean because they're friends."

"Aye. Right you are," the Gnome said.

The steps stopped at a cliff face. A level pathway turned ninety degrees and led through a crevice in the side of the mountain. Dorothy and her friends made their way along the path, turning sideways and squeezing between walls of rock when the course demanded it. The outdoor path turned into a tunnel. An unlit torch hung in a rusty bracket at the shaft's entrance. Sput pulled it from the bracket and retrieved a match from his pocket. He raised one leg and raked the match on the seat of his pants. The match ignited and Sput lit the torch. He turned to Dorothy and Nargoul. "A good Gnome is always prepared to light a fire. You can tell yer granny that."

Holding the torch high, Sput led them into the throat of the mountain, Dorothy close behind him, the others following. They tramped through the tunnel and came to a spacious cavern. A natural bridge extended over a canyon and connected to a broad shelf on the opposite side. Spud, Nargoul and Dorothy stopped before stepping onto the bridge. The others drew close behind them. They looked around the massive grotto. The Gnomes nudged each other and whispered among themselves.

Sput took off his hat and clutched it in his hands. He gazed down in the dark void, the hat shaking in his trembling grip. Pity pricked Dorothy's heart. She stepped up to the anxious Gnome.

"Okay, Sput," Dorothy said. "You've had your turn at leading. Now, it's mine. Give me the torch."

Sput looked up at her, his forehead moist. He handed her the torch. "You know, Kansas. I wuz justa thinkin' that I should step back and defer fer a while. You know, so's nobody gets the notion that I see myself as the shiniest coin in the purse."

With the blazing stick extended above her head, she stepped onto the bridge and then looked back at the group. "Alright. One after the other now. Put one hand on the shoulder of the person in front of you. And no looking down!"

And so, single file, just as Dorothy had instructed, the Crag Lurchers and Gnomes followed her over the viaduct. Not a single Gnome looked down until they reached the platform on the other side.

"I'm a tall amount glad to be over that bridge," one of the Gnomes said.

Another Gnome inhaled through his nostrils and exhaled through his mouth. "If we never see it again, twill be quite alright with me."

The sound of Gnome voices rose inside the cavern as they chatted and laughed, overjoyed that they'd completed the trek across the bridge.

Nargoul raised an open hand. "Everybody quiet!" He cupped a palm behind his ear and listened into the dark distance. "Sounds like metal clinking together."

"I hear it too," Sput said. "Sounds like somebody's ah hammerin' somethin'."

Dorothy pointed. "It's coming from that direction. Let's go!"

Dorothy led the way, the torch blazing. As they walked, the sound of metal clinking grew louder. The walls inside the mountain narrowed to a corridor. Up ahead a dim light pulsated. They made their way down the corridor, the light getting brighter, the pinging of metal getting louder, seasoned with voices and grunts.

The passage opened up to a coliseum-sized room. Fire danced from massive torches stationed throughout the room. Creatures worked like a hill of disturbed ants. They had snouts like aardvarks and noses like pigs. Many of the creatures labored at pushing and pulling carts of rocks along iron tracks. The gold in the rocks sparkled in the torchlight. Other creatures carried baskets and buckets filled with the same. A small minority of the creatures moved among the laborers, cracking leather whips and shouting orders. A worker paused for a moment to wipe the sweat from his forehead. A taskmaster inflicted a painful blow to him with a leather whip.

In the center of the room, a large, muscled being swung a huge hammer, pile driving iron stakes into the cavern floor. With each blow he sheared the rock floor into small pieces. Workers with baskets and buckets gathered up the rocks and dumped them into the carts that the others pulled and pushed. A hefty metal collar fit around the muscled being's neck. A padlock bound the collar to a large chain that connected to a massive iron ball.

Sput bumped Dorothy on the arm with the back of his hand. "Them pig noses are Molewiggins. They're bonfide undesirable and down right despicable. You can tell yer granny that."

A taskmaster growled an order to the hammer-swinger and lashed him with his whip. The captive giant grunted as he heaved the chain, dragging the large iron ball a short distance to an un-shattered portion of cavern floor. He then picked up the great hammer, positioned a stake and resumed pulverizing once again.

Dorothy leaned over to Nargoul. "That must be the Hunchback."

A look of pity flashed on Nargoul's face. "It is, I'm sad to say. It's a shame to see him like this."

Dorothy narrowed her eyes and pressed her lips together, contemplating. Then, it hit her—a plan. She looked at Sput. "Sput, are you up for the Okie Dokie test of all Okie Dokie tests?"

Sput clenched his fists and stuck out his chest. "I'm a Gnome, ain't I?"

Dorothy grinned.

She turned to the others and motioned with her hand. The Crag Luchers and Gnomes drew in close, their full attention on Dorothy.

"Okay, everyone," she said. "Here's what we're gonna do."

Perched in the darkness on a high ledge inside the cavern, the Guardian Owl watched as Dorothy and her friends planned their attack.

Chapter Fourteen

Dorothy and Sput waited in the shadows where the track snaked along one wall of the mountain's spacious grotto. With his head down, an oblivious Molewiggin pushed a mining cart closer and closer to them. The cart's iron wheels clickety-clacked as they rolled along the rails.

"Psst. Hey, you," Sput said in a tone little more than a whisper.

The startled Molewiggin stopped pushing and looked up. When his eyes landed on Sput and Dorothy, he went rigid. He began backing away.

Sput stepped forward, holding out his hand. "No, wait. Wait. We're friends. Lookie here. See what I've got."

The Molewiggin looked to the right then to the left. He walked closer and peered into the hat. Honey and two bricks of comb filled it almost to the brim. The façade of the thick sweet golden liquid casts its spell. The creature's snout twitched as he snorted, licking his jowls.

Sput turned and rotated the hat so that the honey glistened in the torchlight. "Want some?"

"Yeah, yeah," the Molewiggin said, his voice wet and queasy.

"Okay then. Follow me."

Sput started backing farther into the dimness. The Molewiggin followed as if being pulled by a rope. Once the Molewiggin was clear from the view of his fellow laborers, two Gnomes stepped from behind a stalagmite. They spun bolas over their heads in lasso fashion and let them go. The bolas sliced through the air like fan blades. One swirled around the Molewiggin's feet, the other around his torso and arms. In an instant the fettered creature collapsed to the ground.

Houstess, Harlice and two Gnomes rushed over. Harlice held the Molewiggin's mouth shut while one of the Gnomes wrapped it with another bola. Houstess gave a signal to Dorothy and Sput. Harlice, Houstess and the two Gnomes dragged the bound Molewiggin over to the stalagmite and hid him behind it. Three Gnomes unloaded the rocks out of the cart. Dorothy and Sput climbed inside and scrunched down out of sight. The wheels screeched and clanged along the rails as Nargoul, with his head lowered, pushed the cart back toward the noisy mining activity.

"Okay," Dorothy said to Sput. "I'm guessing that once we've freed the Hunchback, we're pretty much in the clear. He must be more than the Molewiggins can handle or they wouldn't have him chained to that iron ball. You'll have to keep them distracted long enough for me to get the key from whichever one has it. Once I do, I'll still need a little more time to unlock the lock. Got it?"

"Got it, Kansas. And don't you go worryin' none. I'll make them hog-nosed varmints dance a jig if need be. You can tell yer granny that."

Nargoul kept his head down as he pushed the cart closer and closer to the place where the Hunchback hammered, the carts wheels clickety-clacking like a phonograph needle hung on a scratched album. The servant Molewiggins labored at their monotonous routines. Pushing. Pulling. Toting. Loading. Unloading. Their expressions empty and numb.

"Okay. Get ready. We're almost there," Nargoul said.

Dorothy and Sput exchanged nods. Nargoul stopped the cart near the Hunchback. Sput climbed out of the cart. The taskmaster Molewiggin that bossed the great hammer swinger reached for his whip. He cracked it in the air and raised it high above his head.

Sput nudged the taskmaster on the back of his leg. "Hey, Hognose. Look what I've got."

The Molewiggin flinched and spun around on his heels. Sput held out his honey-filled hat. The sight enchanted the lust of the loathsome being, his eyes fixed in hypnotic fashion.

"Drop yer whip and follow me," Sput said.

The bewitched Molewiggin concurred, licking his jaws and snorting as he stepped.

"Now, I ain't givin' you the smidgenest of a taste, till you tell me the whereabouts of the key that fits the lock on the big smasher's neck. You do that and you can have honey till it runs out yer floppy ears."

The creature reached a boney-fingered hand into the pouch that hung about his waist. Without removing his eyes from the honey, he pulled out the key.

Sput motioned his head toward Dorothy. "Give it to her."

The Molewiggin extended his hand to Dorothy, the key lying in his opened palm. Dorothy climbed out of the cart. Walked over to him and took the key.

Sput grinned. "Did you see how easy that wuz, Kansas. I tole ye I could charm this repulsive swine of a baboon of a thing."

A raspy voice resonated throughout the cavern. "We have intruders!"

Dorothy and Sput looked up to a ledge where a potbellied Molewiggin stood, his skeletal index finger pointed at them. His brow drawn down. His gnarly teeth displayed. The weight of his voice snapped the Molewiggin out of his honey-enticed trance. The glistening amber illusion inside Sput's hat began to dull. Work inside the cave ceased and all focused their attention on Sput and Dorothy.

Sput look down at the hat in time to see the last semblance of honey fade. He gave the once hypnotized Molewiggin a sheepish look, swallowed hard and returned the hat to his head. The Hunchback lowered his hammer to the floor and turned to look on. The pudgy Molewiggin jumped down to the floor and lumbered over, his flabby belly shifting from side to side with each stride of his scraggy legs. He drew near to Dorothy, Sput andNargoul. The other Molewiggins gathered in to look on.

"A trickster. A falsifying practitioner of hat tomfooleries. That's what you are, Gnome," he said, peering at Sput. "Your sleight of hand will get you nowhere with me." He gritted his teeth as a blob of greenish slime seeped from one of his nostrils. He sucked the wad of snot back into his skull, hacked it into his mouth and chewed it. He cocked his neck to look at Dorothy and Nargoul then spat the clump near Dorothy's feet.

"You have two collaborators, I see," the Molewiggin said. He reached out a hand and slipped his palm under one of Dorothy's locks. "And just WHAT kind of being is this?" He brought the hair to his snout and sniffed it. His breath contaminated the air around Dorothy's face. The juices in her stomach churned; the saliva in her mouth felt warm and thick. She fought back the urge to vomit and jerked away from his touch.

The Molewiggin laughed. "I like a fiery spirit. Comes in handy down here."

He pointed to Nargoul. "Do you know what this is, boys?"

Another Molewiggin yelled from the crowd. "Looks like a feast if you ask me! Let's gut and roast him!"

The obese one shook his head. "No. You roast him and you'll ruin the meat. He'll shrivel up like a dry coconut and be tougher than a unicorn's horn." He looked Nargoul in the eyes and smiled. "Isn't that right?"

Nargoul maintained eye contact and sighed. "I can't say. I've never been cooked before. But the fire couldn't make me as vile to the eye as you are."

The fat Molewiggin shut his eyes, dropped his head and brought a fist to his chest. "Now, that hurts me clean to the heart." He pretended to cry, then opened his eyes and looked at Nargoul. "But I think I'll recover." He laughed mockingly.

He turned to the crowd. "You see, boys, this is a Crag Lurcher. Some mighty fine eating when you boil them. The meat just falls off the bones." He fluttered his fingers in the air.

The Molewiggins grunted and snorted.

The fat one raised his hands to quiet them. "But you know what really makes the meat tasty?"

The mob reveled at his question, then calmed back down to listen.

The Molewiggin reached down and picked Sput up by the collar of his shirt and held him up for all to see. "When you boil them with Gnomes! Crag Lurcher and Gnome stew is food fit for a king!"

The Molewiggins erupted in grunts and howls. The obese one tossed Sput to the ground next to Nargoul and Dorothy. When the noise of the crowd died down, he pointed to Dorothy. "We'll throw this long-haired one in and see how she makes the pot taste!" He spread his hand high over his head. "Search every crack and shaft. I'm sure there's more in our midst! Find them, boys, and we'll sleep with full bellies tonight."

At the command of the plump superior, some of the Molewiggins crowded in and began binding Dorothy, Nargoul and Sput. The others commenced a fixated search of the inside of the cave.

Linmar shot out of Dorothy's pocket and darted over to the Hunchback. The crafty chipmunk scurried up the chain to the padlock and jetted into the keyhole. Within minutes the Molewiggins had rounded up the Gnomes and Crag Lurchers. With pointed sticks and gruesome iron tools, they corralled them to the center of the cavern.

"Fire up the pots!" the fatso yelled.

With snorts and squeals of hungry anticipation, Molewiggins gathered wood and straw and piled it under two large iron pots that hung suspended under tripods. They then formed a bucket brigade and filled the pots with water drawn from a nearby fissure. A one-eyed Molewiggin grabbed a torch and tossed it on the kindling mound. The blaze swept through the heap. The Molewiggins' empty wrinkled eye socket looked like an embedded spider on his face in the fire's light. The fire's heat began to pat Dorothy on her cheeks and forehead.

"Hurry! Toss 'em in before the water starts boiling!" the big-bellied one said. "Makes for amusing entertainment before eating! And, start with the longhair! Let's see how much spirit she really has!" He laughed, holding his flabby midsection.

Two Molewiggins grabbed Dorothy and wrestled her toward the pots.

Nargoul lunged toward them. "Take your hands off her or I'll—"

A leather strap tethered around his ankles and he crashed to the ground. He rolled over and looked up. A Molewiggin taskmaster stood over him, holding the handle of his whip. He glared at Nargoul, his eyes narrowed and hateful. "Show some manners or we'll skin you alive first."

The two lifted Dorothy up to toss her in when the giant iron ball crashed down onto the pots. The impact smashed the tripods, spilled the water and extinguished the fire. With Linmar on one shoulder, the rampaging Hunchback tossed carts, sections of track and crossties throughout the cave room. Dorothy, the Crag Lurchers and the Gnomes watched as the Molewiggins scrambled for their lives.

"We're safe now! They're no match for the Hunchback!" Nargoul said. "Look at them run!"

"I'm gladder'na horsefly on the hind end of a bison to have him on our side! You can tell yer granny that!" Sput said with a wink and smile.

Gnomes hurried over and untied Dorothy, Sput and Nargoul. Abandoned whips, spears, and tools lay around the floor, not a single Molewiggin to be found.

The Hunchback looked down at the three Round-eyes and smiled. "Hello fellas. It's great to see you again. Thanks for freeing me."

Harlice pointed to Dorothy. "You can thank her."

The Hunchback bent down to make eye contact with Dorothy. "Who might you be?"

"My name's Dorothy. I'm from a place called Kansas."

"And, the black on your mouth? Is it—"

"Yes. It's Devil's Spit," Dorothy said.

The Hunchback scratched his massive baldhead. "I don't understand. Where the mark is, evil dwells inside. But, you're not evil. You're good or you wouldn't have risked your life to save me."

"Well, I think I'm far from good, but let's just say I'm working at it."

"She's on a mission to break the spell of the Nesterclop," said Nargoul. "We came along to help."

The Hunchback looked at Nargoul and raised his eyebrows.

"It's true," Houstess said. "She can do it."

The Hunchback turned back to Dorothy and reached out a massive hand for a shake. Dorothy obliged, a big smile on her face.

"I'm known in this land as the Hunchback. But my friends call me Hunch. I'm forever indebted to you, Dorothy. What can I do to help?"

"I'd be grateful if you'd go back to Rantoul Grove so you can release the water when my mission's complete.'

The Hunchback rapped a clenched fist over one knee, his eyes large. "You don't mean it?"

"Absolutely! That's why we came here to get you."

"Nothing would make me happier," Hunch said. "It's my great purpose in life ya know. I'd come to believe that I'd never see my mountain again. That I'd have to break rocks for the Molewiggins forever."

"It won't be easy," Dorothy said. "We'll have to take the mountain from Skurtz. He lives there now. He's a Scaithe."

Hunch drew his brow down and displayed his teeth. "I hate Scaithes."

Linmar jumped from Hunch's shoulder to his knee, then to the ground. Dorothy reached down and offered her hand to her furry partner. She raised him up close to her face and looked at him. She stroked him between the eyes with a finger.

"It would have been the pots for all of you if it hadn't been for that little fella," Hunch said. "He somehow unlocked the collar that bound me."

Dorothy looked up at Hunch. "He has a knack for coming through at just the right time."

She returned Linmar to her pocket.

"Okay, Hunch. Think you can lead us to Rantoul Grove? We've got a job to do," she said.

"It'd be my pleasure."

Dorothy, the Crag Lurchers and the Gnomes followed as the giant led them to their next destination. Rantoul Grove.

Chapter Fifteen

The trees of Rantoul Grove clawed into the sky like parched skeletons buried with their forearms and hands sticking out of the ground. Hissing wind rolled tumbleweeds on the barren soil of the ghastly landscape. Dorothy and her friends surveyed the lifeless scene, following along behind the Hunchback.

Sput looked up into the tops of the trees. "If ole Satan himself has a sticker bush orchard," he said. "I guarantee ye it's a beauty to behold compared to this place."

Just up the road, a rotund tree grew on the side of the grove's only peak. A lone raven cawed from the tree's uppermost branch.

"We're almost at my cave," Hunch said.

Dorothy wrenched her face as if smelling something putrid. "You call this place home?"

Hunch stopped. Put his hands on his hips. "If only you could've seen it before," he said, scanning the landscape. "It was beautiful . . . until the Nesterclop tricked me."

"How'd he do that?" Dorothy asked.

Hunch shook his head and exhaled. "By talking . . . just by talking. He can say things in ways to make you believe him and trust him. The water no longer flows in the land." The big creature lowered his head. "And it's all because I listened to him."

"We don't hold it against you, Hunch," Nargoul said. "We know how sinister the Nesterclop is. Crag Lurchers are divided today because of his underhanded ways."

Sput turned to the group. "I wish he'uz here right now." He raised the Wardin Staff. "I'd put the crook on his neck and send'im to the black lake." He plunged the end of the staff down on the ground and huffed. "And you can tell yer granny that."

"But why?" Dorothy asked. "Why does he do such horrible things?"

"It's his nature," Nargoul said. "It's who he is."

"No love in him," Harlice said. "No light. Only darkness."

"Kill. Steal. Destroy," Houstess said. "That's all he wants to do."

"That's rather melodramatic. But then again, you are Round-eyes," came a tantalizing voice from nearby.

Dorothy and her friends turned to look.

A copper-toned, smooth-skinned, man flashed a brilliant smile as he leaned against a tree, his hands in the pockets of his orange trousers. He stood and walked toward them. "It's been a long time, Hunchback," the man said, looking up at the massive being.

The man pulled a comb from inside his tuxedo jacket and raked it through his already perfect black hair as he came closer.

Dorothy tightened her eyelids. "I know him. He's the—"

"He's the Nesterclop." Houstess finished Dorothy's sentence.

The Nesterclop shot Dorothy a broad smile. "Ah, Dorothy. So, we meet again. You've been practicing the motto so I hear. Your craftiness at the depot left quite the impression I must say."

He raked through his hair again. "And, that little episode with the Gem-fairy princess." He tilted the comb toward her. "Now that was sheer artistry."

He returned it to the inside pocket of his jacket then glanced at her, his smile replaced by a stern expression. "But what I'm hearing lately causes me concern. So, I thought it time for you and I to have . . . might I say . . . a refocusing session."

Dorothy stepped forward. "My focus is fine. I'm done with the motto and anything else that might come out of your sinister mouth."

The Nesterclop clicked his tongue and shook his head. "You HAVE softened. Disappointing. Very disappointing." He drew close to her, his sparkling eyes changing colors like before, the familiar scent of his cologne seasoning the air around Dorothy's face. "You should hear my deal before becoming my foe. After all, I do know where Toto is."

Dorothy's heart sank in her chest. "Really?"

He winked. "Yes indeed."

The Nesterclop stood erect and examined his fingernails. "But he's in such a strenuous dilemma that you'll never get him back without my help."

Nargoul stepped up next to Dorothy and touched her arm with the back of his hand. "He's trying to charm you. Remember who you are and what your mission is."

"That's right, Kansas," Sput said. "Them's okie dokie-in' words he's speakin'. Keep yer wits about che."

Dorothy didn't acknowledge them, her attention locked on the Nesterclop. "What's your deal?"

The Nesterclop smiled. "A wise one you are, Dorothy. Only a fool declines a deal before hearing about the payoff. Now, my deal is heavily slanted in your favor. I'll get your dog back for you and then see to it that both of you are on you way back Kansas before nightfall."

"Please, Dorothy. Don't listen to him! It's a trap I tell you!" Hunch said.

The Nesterclop closed his eyes and pressed his lips together. He breathed out a heavy breath through his nose and looked at Hunch. "I advise you to stay out of this, Water-keeper. Of her own will, she asked to hear the deal. Therefore, she's entitled to my offer. You interfere and you'll pay the consequence." He scanned the faces of the Gnomes and Crag Lurchers. "That goes for the rest of you as well.

The Nesterclop turned his attention back to Dorothy. "If you want Toto back and you want to return to Kansas, I'm the one who can make these things happen," he said and thumbed his chest. "All I ask in return is—"

Hunch hammered the air with his fists at his sides. "Dorothy, don't believe him! It's a trap I tell you! A trap! I'm sure of it!"

"I gave you fair warning, Water-keeper," the Nesterclop said. He reached his hand inside the lapel of his jacket and pulled out a large metal ring.

Hunch began to tremble.

The Nesterclop held it up before him. "Look at it closely now. Notice that it is one solid ring of metal." He rotated the ring and turned it from side to side. "Its metal is unbreakable. Notice how brilliant it shines. And, here's the best part. It's uniquely crafted for your thick neck . . . to render you weak!"

He snapped the fingers on his other hand. In an instant the ring appeared on Hunch's neck. The Nesterclop made a backhand motion in the air and a force unseen moved Hunch to one side and pinned him against the trunk of a tree.

"You thought breaking rocks for the Molewiggins was burdensome," the Nesterclop said, a cool look on his face. "When you see what I have planned for you, you'll beg me to let you go back to that hammer."

He turned his attention to the Gnomes and Crag Luchers and fanned an intimidating index finger in their direction. "Would anyone else wish to protest?"

They all held silent.

The Nesterclop opened his hand toward Sput. "I'll be taking that annoying stick of yours."

The Warding Staff pulled out of Sput's hand and shot into the hand of the Nesterclop.

He looked at Dorothy, his eyes sparkling as they did during her first encounter. And, just as before, she felt the charm of his presence. "Never mind them," he said, shaking his head, the corners of his mouth turned down. "They're hindering you. If you want Toto and you want to get back to Kansas all you have to do is forget this silly business about breaking a so-called curse. It's nonsense. Absolute nonsense. This land is not under a curse. Things are now as they've always been."

The Nesterclop motioned toward the group. "Look at them, Dorothy. They're not like you and me—intelligent—strong—dominating—progressing," he said, his words caressing her ego. "They're oddities and questionables. A mix and match hodge podge of repulsive hybrids, mutations and simpletons."

Dorothy glanced at the faces of the Crag Lurchers and Gnomes.

The Nesterclop took Dorothy's chin and turned her face back to his. "You can't depend on the likes of them. And, the most unreliable of all of them is that shunned jail keeper, Zimboza. He's demented. This curse-breaking notion he's put in your head is a pile of sawdust." He released her chin. "A sensational, drummed up lie. Stick with me." He tapped his chest. "I can give you what you want. So, what do you say? Do we have a deal?"

He extended his left hand for a handshake.

"Can I have a moment to think about it?"

The Nesterclop bowed and raised an open palm. "Certainly," he said with a thin smile.

Dorothy studied the faces of Gnomes and Crag Lurchers. Sput tightened his lips and sighed. Harlice and Houstess slumped, their faces drooping with sadness. Nargoul closed his eyes and lowered his head.

Dorothy crossed her arms over her stomach and paced back and forth. Linmar bolted from her pocket as if blasted out of a gun. He darted over to Hunch and scurried up one of his legs and onto the giant's shoulder. He made a squeaking sound that got Dorothy's attention. She turned on her heels to look. Standing on his hind legs, the peculiar chipmunk peered into Dorothy's eyes. With one of his tiny paws, he tapped Hunch on the side of the face.

Okay. So why did Linmar want her to focus on Hunch? What did the used-to-be water keeper have to do with her decision? Wait a minute. Water keeper . . . water keeper—that was it. The Nesterclop had referred to Hunch as the water keeper. Before being kidnapped by the Nesterclop and the Scaithes, Hunch used to govern the flow of water throughout the land of the Red Brick Road. Things WERE different then. The land used to live and thrive. The Nesterclop was lying. He was out only to kill, steal and destroy. Just like Houstess had said. Dorothy smiled at Linmar. Once again, her loyal little friend had helped her avoid a hazard.

Dorothy turned back to the Nesterclop. "I'd like very much to have Toto at my side and be back in Kansas."

The Nesterclop offered his hand once again for a shake. "Now, that's what I was hoping to hear."

Dorothy raised an open hand in the direction of the Crag Lurchers and Gnomes then toward Hunch. "These, you say, are oddities and questionables. Well, I know them to be genuine and brave. The best friends anyone could ask for. They've risked their lives to help me get this far. They've stuck with me so I'm sticking with them. Friends don't turn their backs on each other no matter how good a new deal might seem. So, no deal!"

The Nesterclop's beautiful eyes turned to those of a fiery serpent. He spread his lips in scorn, his once brilliant smile now a ghastly display of gnarly teeth with fangs.

"Very well, then!" he said with a graveled voice.

He snapped his fingers. An army of Molewiggins emerged from behind the surrounding trees. "Looks like you'll be having a feast after all, boys," he said. "You can have the Crag Lurchers and the Gnomes for your pots. They're useless to me. But the Hunchback and the headstrong she-ling are mine."

The Molewiggins rushed in, snorting and shrieking in anticipation. In the midst of the commotion Linmar jumped from Hunch's shoulder and dashed to the Nesterclop. He bolted up the back of the Nesterclop's leg and under the tail of his jacket. In a flash he emerged from under his collar. Linmar sank his teeth deep into the Nesterclop's neck. The Nesterclop let out a painful growl and dropped the Warding Staff. He reached up, pulled Linmar from his punctured neck, and threw him to the ground. With clinched teeth and a grimacing face, he raised one foot over the chipmunk and drove his heel down hard. Linmar squealed. The Nesterclop twisted his foot, grinding Dorothy's loyal little friend into the hard soil.

"Linmar!" Dorothy yelled.

The Nesterclop lifted his foot from Linmar's injured body.

Blood oozed from the chipmunk's tiny nose. Laying on his side, he pulled himself toward Dorothy. Dragging his disfigured back legs.

Dorothy ran over and stooped down to pick him up. As she reached out to take him in her hand, the Nesterclop drove his foot down on the chipmunk a second time. He shifted, transferring all his weight to the foot that pinned Linmar to the ground.

"No! No! No!" Dorothy cried out.

The Nesterclop slowly raised his foot, his facial expression displaying hellish jubilation. Linmar lay motionless, his eyes shut.

Dorothy cried out. "He was only trying to protect me!"

She scooped up the mangled creature with her cupped palms. "Oh, Linmar, my brave and loyal friend, please don't die. Please be okay."

Dorothy rolled Linmar's limp body over to one hand then to the other. Dead. Dorothy couldn't image even the death of her beloved Toto paining her heart more. A drop of blood trickled through her fingers. Dorothy's chin quivered. Her eyes welled. She felt the sudden empty place in her soul—the place once occupied by Linmar. He was gone . . . because of her. Sadness morphed into guilt. Her thoughts reached back to the recent past. The Gem-fairy princess was dead because of HER. The elderly gentleman from the depot was dead because of HER.

The Nesterclop turned to the Molewiggins. "We're finished here. Do with the smalls as you wish. I'll be on my way with the Hunchback and the girl."

The Molewiggins began herding away the Crag Lurchers and Gnomes. Dorothy stood like a statue, gazing through tears at Linmar's lifeless body. The Nesterclop bent down and grasped the Warding Staff. He raised to the sight of a glowing, magnificent blade. His expression melted to fright.

"Drop it," a voice said.

Dorothy's heart fluttered. She snapped out of her zone and shot her head up.

She looked on with wide eyes as the boy walked toward the Nesterclop, brandishing a sword.

The Nesterclop dropped the Warding Staff. "As you wish."

The boy drew close to the Nesterclop and leaned the tip of the metal to the side of his face. The Nesterclop raised his open hands. "We both know I'm no match for the Sword of Jerubaal. Granted, I must submit to your demands. But you can't take my life. This is but the first time the blade's been wielded to my throat. So, I'll just be on my way."

The Nesterclop lowered his head and took a step back. He touched his forehead with the fingertips of one hand and gave the boy a departing salute.

The boy stepped toward him and touched the edge of the blade to the Nesterclop's cheek once again. "Unshackle the Hunchback and call off the Molewiggins or I'll gash your smooth face."

"Of course. You have the sword so you're the boss."

The Nesterclop waved a hand toward the Molewiggins. "You heard him! Release them!"

Like hyenas retracting from a male lion, the Molewiggins withdrew from the Crag Lurchers and Gnomes.

"There. Just as you requested," the Nesterclop said, a bead of sweat sliding down his nose. "

The boy stuck the tip of the sword in one of the Nesterclop's nostrils. "The Hunchback!"

The Nesterclop looked down at the blade and cracked a grin. "Oh, yes. How could I forget?"

Dorothy watched the exchange, her heart fluttering as the fearless boy handled the Nesterclop like a potter manipulating wet clay.

The Nesterclop snapped his fingers again and the ring fell from Hunch's neck and onto the ground.

Hunch rubbed his throat where the irritating ring had been and looked at the boy. "Thanks," he said.

The boy nodded and lowered the blade of the sword to his side. "There now. I think we're all square. Are we not?" the Nesterclop said, his tone sheepish.

The boy lifted his chin and smirked. "We're never square," he said. "But be gone nonetheless!"

The Nesterclop backed away a few paces. He flicked a wrist and a black top hat appeared in his hand. He positioned the hat on his head, turned and started walking.

When he came to the metal ring, he stopped and looked over his shoulder. "May I?"

The boy nodded once again.

The Nesterclop reached down, picked up the ring and returned it to the inside of his coat. "After all, it is mine." He stood up, tugged on his lapels to tidy himself and walked away.

Nargoul stepped up to the boy. "Are we ever glad to see you!"

"Gen-u-ine-ly. You can tell yer granny that." Sput reached out his hand to the boy for a shake. "My name's Clyde Erskine Sweetwater Festerburton the Third. But you can call me—"

"Sput," the boy said and cracked a confident smile as he shook Sput's hand.

"How'd you know my name?"

The looked Sput in the eyes and maintained his smile.

"I thought we were stew for sure," Houstess said.

Harlice shrugged his shoulders, his open palms turned upward. "How did you know where to find us?"

The boy pointed to the top of a nearby tree where the Guardian Owl sat perched on a limb. The owl gave a slow, deliberate blink.

The boy held out his hand to Dorothy. "Give him to me."

Dorothy laid Linmar's motionless body in the boy's palm. The boy placed Linmar's body on the ground. Then, with the diligence and focus of a surgeon, he placed the tip of the sword over Linmar's heart.

Dorothy lunged forward. "Oh, no! Please don't!"

Nargoul grabbed Dorothy by her dress sleeve. "Don't worry. Trust and watch."

The end of the Sword of Jerubaal glowed. A dome of light covered Linmar. The chipmunk jerked several times, took a deep breath and opened his eyes. The arc of light disappeared and the tip of the blade returned to normal. Linmar stretched as if waking from a deep sleep then stood up on his hind legs.

Dorothy's eyes shot open. "I can't believe it! You've healed him and brought him back to life!"

She stooped down and reached out her hand. Linmar jumped into it, ran up her arm and disappeared into her pocket.

Dorothy stood. "Thank you. Oh, thank you. I thought I'd lost him forever!"

"The Nesterclop will leave you alone for now," the boy said. "But he'll be watching for another opportunity. I suggest you get a move on." He looked up at the owl and then back at Dorothy. "I must be on my way."

He turned and walked into the leafless woods.

Dorothy gazed at him. "Thanks again!"

The boy waved a hand in the air without looking back and kept walking.

Sput picked up the Warding Staff and looked at Dorothy with one eye closed. "This is where we Gnomes do our part. So, with your permission, Kansas, we'll take care of that thieving Scaithe."

The other Gnomes joined in with hardy agreement.

"Permission granted. Bring him to me," Dorothy said.

"Okay, fellers, keep yer hands on yer bolas. We's going Scaithe huntin'," Sput said and headed into the cave. The other Gnomes fell in behind him.

"Confronting a Scaithe is no easy task," Hunch said. "Do you think those Gnomes will be okay by themselves?"

"They'll be fine," Dorothy said.

A faint smile stretched on Nargoul's face, his eyes fixed on the mouth of the cave. "A Scaithe doesn't stand a chance against a Gnome with the Warding Staff."

· ·

Purple light beamed from the mouth of the cave. Sput strolled out, a confident smile on his face, his chest forward. Skurtz lumbered after him, his chin down, his shoulders relaxed. Behind Skurtz, a Gnome marched, holding the crook of the Warding Staff just above the base of Skurt's skull.

Sput pointed to the ground in front of Dorothy. "On yer knees over there you repulsatin' varmint."

Skurtz walked over to where Dorothy stood and dropped to his knees. He cowered before her as the Gnome held the bend of the staff above his head, the gleaming purple stone almost touching one of his pointed ears.

"Look at me," Dorothy said.

Skurtz raised his head slowly, his chin quivering.

Dorothy bore her eyes into his. "Where is it?"

Skurtz reached into the pouch that hung at his waist and pulled out the Gem-fairy's ring. He lowered his head again and held the gleaming jewel up to Dorothy. She took it from his hand and dropped it in the pocket of her dress.

Skurtz brought his hands together in front of his chest and interlocked his fingers. "Please, Dorothy. I beg you. Grant me my life and you'll never see me again. Nor will anyone else in the land of the Red Brick Road."

Dorothy scanned the faces of her comrades. Hunch curled one side of his mouth. The Crag Lurchers shook their heads.

"He'll be loyal to the Nesterclop wherever he goes," Nargoul said.

Sput folded his arms and cocked his head to one side. "Once a Scaithe always a Scaithe. And you can tell yer granny that."

Dorothy looked down at Skurtz. "You're right. I'll never see you again and neither will anyone else around here because you'll be at the bottom of the black lake."

Skurtz let out a shrill cry. "No! No! Please!"

Dorothy cut her eyes to the Gnome holding the Warding Staff and nodded. The Gnome hooked the curved end of the staff around Skurtz's neck, the purple gem giving off arcs of violet light.

Skurtz's skin began turning to dry leather as it tightened to his skeleton. His head tilted back and his mouth opened as if invisible hands were prying his jaws apart. His malignant spirit exited his jagged, cavernous mouth. It lifted above the treetops and bolted through the sky.

Dorothy and her friends watched as the Scaithe's carcass shrank and steamed until it was no more.

Sput looked at Dorothy, grinned and winked. "Okay, Kansas, that Scaithe's done fer. You won't see tooth, fang or claw of him again. He's bound for the depths of the Devil's Spit Spot. You can tell yer granny that."

Dorothy turned to Hunch. "Well, you know what that means, Hunch. Now, you can occupy the cave. What was once yours is now yours again."

Linmar stuck his head out of Dorothy's pocket.

Hunch looked around at all of them. "I could never thank you enough."

"Seeing the water flow throughout the land again will be thanks enough," Houstess said.

"And the sooner the better," Harlice added.

Hunch grinned. "Then I'd better get started. I'm sure I have a lot of work to do."

He started backing toward the mouth of the cave, thanking them and waving as he went.

With his mouth half-opened Houstess nudged Nargoul and Harlice on their shoulders. "Look! Did you see that?"

"I sure did!" Harlice said.

"What? What are you talking about?" Dorothy asked.

"The Devil's Spit," Nargoul said. "Some of it just faded from your face."

Nargoul raised an index finger. "Think about it. When you complete the remainder of the mission, it'll all be gone."

Dorothy smiled. "It's really happening. Just like Zimboza said. The curse is being broken. I'd better get going. I still have a lot left to do."

Harlice nodded. "We'll come with you."

Nargoul shook his head, his lips pressed together. "We can't, Harlice."

"What do you mean, 'We can't.'"

"He's right, Harlice," Houstess said. "Dorothy has to accomplish three tasks. Remember what the oracle said. Friends can help her with the first one, but the other two she has to do on her own."

"What are you going to do next?" Nargoul asked.

Dorothy drew her brow down. "The first task was to return that which once was stolen. We just did that for Hunch. Zimboza said the second thing I must do is show love to the unlovable. Hmm. Who is the most unlovable in all the land of the Red Brick Road?"

Nargoul, Houstess and Harlice exchanged looks and shook their heads.

"Let's come up with someone else," Harlice said.

Houstess looked at Nargoul. "I agree with Harlice. We should come up with someone else."

Dorothy stepped up to them. "It's obvious that you're all thinking of the same person."

Nargoul sighed. "Endora."

Dorothy paused for a moment. "Then, Endora it is."

Sput pushed his hat up on his head and threw his shoulders back. "That talkin'less woman that lives in Nimrod's Swamp! She's meaner'na rattlin' flathead serpent."

Houstess shrugged his shoulders, his palms turned up. "How are you going to show her love?"

Dorothy started pacing. "I don't know how exactly. At least not right now. I'll figure it out when the time comes." She put her hands on her hips. "I figure it'll be like walking at night holding a torch."

"What in tarnation do you mean, Kansas?" Sput said.

"You can walk a long way with a torch, but you can see only enough to take a few steps at a time. But, if you keep taking those few steps, before you know it, you've walked all the way to town," Dorothy said. "I think that's the approach I'm gonna take."

"Don't forget to give them to her, Sput," one of the Gnomes said.

Sput swung a fist in the air. "Oh yeah. I plum near forgot. Thanks for reminding me." He looked at Dorothy. "We have a little gift for you, Kansas." He turned to one of the Gnomes. "Danworth, give 'em to her."

Danworth stepped out from the group of Gnomes, holding a pair of leather moccasins. Sput pushed his hat up on his head. "Some of the fellers've been workin' on these while we've been questin' here and yonder. Them fancy shoes you're wearin' can't be very tolerable on rugged terrain. Maybe these'll come in handy when yer doin' yer off-road venturin' Besides they'll help you not to forget us."

Dorothy took the moccasins from Danworth and studied them. Soft on the inside. They'd prove useful.

"How could I ever forget you," she said. "With all your bravery and Scaithe banishing and okie-dokie-ing."

The Gnomes blushed with pride, elbowing, nodding and winking at each other.

"And the same goes for you Round-eyes. You left your families and risked your lives for me. More loyal friends one could never find."

"When your mission is accomplished come see us at the gorge. Will you?" Harlice said.

"You can count on it."

"We'll be rootin' for you, Kansas. You can tell yer granny that."

"Well, I guess that's about it. I better get going," Dorothy said and set out on her way to Nimrod's Swamp . . . to find Endora.

. . . .

"Dorothy from Kansas. I hope your mission is nearing completion," Zimboza mused. He peered out over the dry river bottom. Narrow-eyes lay along the banks, their bellies swelling and deflating as they slept the great sleep of the Guardian Owl's spell. Zimboza looked down at the dogwood blossom he held. Two petals remained.

Chapter Sixteen

Dimness matured to darkness as the sun sank behind the horizon. Dorothy walked along the Red Brick Road, the heels of the slippers clicking on the cobblestones with each of her steps. How would she find Endora? Would Dorothy have to leave the road and lumber through the murky, uninviting bayou? Would Endora come out and ambush Dorothy? Could it be that Endora was already stalking her from the swamp's trees and thick foliage? How might Dorothy show love to the notorious tongue-less woman? Endora's heart was as black as coal, no doubt. And twice as hard. Would it soften with an act of benevolence or would Dorothy's tongue end up in Endora's boiling pot?

Up ahead on the road a small light glowed. Dorothy stopped. A lantern, perhaps? Maybe even Endora's lantern? Dorothy slipped behind a tree and peeked around it. She waited, her heart beating faster as the light came closer. Linmar emerged from her pocket and climbed to her shoulder.

"This could be her, Linmar," she whispered.

The light continued along the road, stopping just beyond Dorothy's hiding place. Dorothy took Linmar from her shoulder and returned him to her pocket. Best to be safe. Endora might have a special taste for chipmunks. Dorothy breathed in deep through her nostrils and exhaled.

Overcome evil with good. Overcome evil with good, Dorothy meditated. She'd heard Pastor Claxton make the statement and similar others over and over again in his Sunday morning sermons. Dorothy often referred to him as Parrot Claxton as the minister was prone to repetition. At this moment, however, she was grateful to her country parson for etching such helpful words into her mind. Dorothy gathered her courage, determined to step out and greet whoever held the light.

"I know you're hiding behind the tree, Dorothy. So, you might as well show yourself," came a familiar voice.

Dorothy shot her eyes open in surprise. Could it be? She sure hoped so.

Dorothy stepped out from behind the tree and looked into the light, her forearm over her brow. The light bearer set his lantern on the red bricks and pulled his pocketknife and the block of wood out of his pocket. He cut a slice and inspected his work in the lamplight.

"What are you doing out here in this swamp?" the boy said, positioning the knife to make another cut.

"I'm looking for Endora," Dorothy said.

The boy stopped mid-stroke and looked up at Dorothy with his eyes but not his head. "You're kidding, right?"

"No."

The boy folded his knife and shoved it back into his pocket along with the piece of wood. "Let me get this straight. First you go toe-to-toe with the Nesterclop and now you come out here looking for Endora. Are you TRYING to get yourself killed?"

"No, I'm TRYING to break the Nesterclop's curse. You had me play Mumbley-peg with you so Zimboza would recognize me."

"You think so, huh?"

"I know so."

"Do you despise me?"

"Not at all. I'm grateful. If it hadn't been for you, I would've gone completely over to the Nesterclop's side."

The boy picked up the lantern and came closer. He held it up high. The light revealed the warm smile on his face.

"Well, alright then," he said. "Back up the road a bit, there's a clean, dry spot. We can build a fire. I've got some food and water. What do you say?"

"I'm starving," Dorothy said. "Haven't had a thing all day."

The two of them walked along the road and came to the dry clearing the boy had mentioned. A circle of stones bordered a cone-shaped pile of wood. Next to it, two fat, short round logs stood on their ends.

The boy motioned. "Have a seat."

Dorothy sat down on one of the logs. The boy pulled a thin stick from the pile and lit it with the flame of the lantern. In moments, a roaring fire illuminated the campsite. The boy snuffed out the lantern and walked a short distance from the fire where a knapsack lay along with a jug of water. He picked them up and walked back to the fire and sat down next to Dorothy.

"You like drumsticks and cornbread?"

Dorothy cocked her head. "Do I ever?"

The boy pulled two drumsticks and a palm-sized piece of cornbread from the satchel. Dorothy reached for them, her eyes bulging.

"And what about oatmeal and raisin cookies? Do you like them too?"

"My favorite!" she said and bit off a chunk of crispy battered chicken.

The boy reached into the knapsack, pulled out one and handed it to her.

"It's strange, but I feel you knew that already somehow."

The boy shrugged and turned over an opened hand. "Now, how could I?"

Dorothy stopped before biting off a piece of the cookies. "Yeah. How could you?"

The boy offered her the jug. "Water?"

Dorothy took it, chugged down a long drink and wiped her mouth with her forearm. "Where's Toto?"

"He's close by."

Dorothy gasped. "Is he? Is he really?" She stood up. "Toto! Toto!"

The boy took a bite of a cookie. "You're wasting your breath. He's not coming to you."

Dorothy continued looking into the dark swamp. "If he can hear me, he'll come running to me."

The boy shook his head.

"He's close, but he can't hear me?"

"He can hear you alright. But he won't come."

Dorothy turned on her heels. "Why not? What have you done to him?"

The boy returned the uneaten portion to the satchel. "He's fine. Trust me."

He pulled out his pocketknife and the piece of wood and started whittling again.

"When will I get him back? I . . . I will get him back. Won't I?" Dorothy sat back down, her chin starting to quiver.

"In time I think you will."

He rotated the wood a few times, examining it. "Yup. I think you will."

"What do you mean, "In time?""

The boy held the piece of wood close to the firelight. "It's getting there." He folded the knife and returned it to his pocket along with the wood. He stood and pushed his hair back with one hand. "I've gotta be going."

"Don't go."

"Got somewhere I have to be. You can have the bag. Cookies are in it."

"Do you have any suggestions on where I might find Endora?"

"You don't have to find her. Just sit here next to the fire and she'll find you. I wouldn't be surprised if she's here before I'm out of the swamp."

He picked up the lantern and shook it to check the fuel level.

"Any advice on how I might . . . you know, be her friend or something?" Dorothy said.

The boy took a flaming twig from the fire and relit the lantern. "Well, she's a girl and you're a girl. I'm sure you'll figure it out."

He trimmed the wick. The lantern glowed at full strength. The boy tossed the stick back on the fire and started walking. Before he stepped onto the Red Brick Road, he stopped and looked back. "I do hope you figure out something. Cause if you don't, she'll have your tongue for sure. You take care now."

Dorothy nodded and the boy walked away. She sat next to the fire and watched the light of the lantern get smaller and smaller as the boy walked farther and farther away from her. Dorothy stuffed a large piece of the cornbread into her mouth. The leftover portion she held just above the top of her pocket. "You hungry, little buddy?"

The sound of her voice and the smell of the morsel aroused the napping Linmar. The loyal chipmunk climbed from the bottom of her pocket and took the bread from her hand. Eager for another cookie, Dorothy reached for the knapsack and plunged a hand inside. The feel of the two rigid objects inside the backpack piqued her curiosity. The cookies could wait. She pulled the items from the bag. A mirror. A hairbrush.

"I don't know whether to be irritated or grateful, Linmar."

She looked in the mirror. For the first time she saw what others in the land saw—a girl with a faced marked by the Devil's Spit. The black that tipped her nose and almost circled her mouth reminded her of who she'd been and what she could be if ever she neglected the lessons she'd learned already. The place on her face where the black had been but no longer was reminded her of who she could be if she forever kept to heart those same lessons.

A triple knock behind her jolted her out of her introspection.

Dorothy jumped to her feet and turned around.

"Who's there?"

Silence. Dorothy stepped away from the fire and edge closer to the direction of the sound. Another triple knock.

"Endora?"

Silence again.

"I'm Dorothy and I want to be your friend! Endora, if that's you knock two times! Please!"

A long pause. Then, two knocks rang out from the darkness.

"I've got some food! Drumsticks! They're really good! And, oatmeal and raisin cookies for dessert! Fresh water too! I've been wanting to meet you!"

Dorothy stood still and looked into the blackness. Part of her hoped that Endora would step out from the shadows and show herself. Part of her dreaded such an encounter. What did a tongue-eating swamp witch look like? How was Endora making the knocking sounds? A spear? A hatchet? A butcher's knife? The stone she'd bash Dorothy's head with just before she'd cut out her tongue and cook it? Dorothy continued to wait . . . and wonder . . . and stare into the damp night air.

But Endora never came forth. And never made another knock. Dorothy took a deep breath. Paused. Then exhaled. She turned to walk back to the campfire and there . . . on the opposite side of the crackling flames . . . stood a woman. The sight of her hit Dorothy like ice in the face. The swamp woman's matted, stringy, mane-like hair hung down almost to her knees. A sleeveless makeshift dress made of animal hide covered her body from the shoulders almost to her ankles. With one hand she held a long spear. With the other she clutched the handle of the large knife sheathed in her belt. Dorothy swallowed hard and gathered her courage.

"You . . . you must be Endora."

Without returning an expression, the odd woman nodded once.

"Would you like something to eat? I've got plenty."

Endora stood still. No reply. Dorothy walked toward the two logs next to the fire. Endora kept her eyes fixed on Dorothy.

Dorothy pointed. "Look! A seat for you and a seat for me."

Endora maintained her fixed gaze as Dorothy took calculated steps toward the campfire, eased herself down on one of the logs and began musing to herself. Act like everything's normal. Make small talk.

"I've been looking for you because I want to be your friend. Honest."

The light of the fire illuminated Dorothy's face. Endora's eyes shot open. She began stepping back, a look of horror on her face. She pointed to Dorothy then touched her finger to her mouth.

"No! No! Don't go away! Please! I can explain."

Endora stopped, her hand now on her knife again.

"I know. It looks terrible. I'm not evil or a Scaithe or anything like that. I got it on my face when I played Mumbley-peg with the boy who's always whittling with a pocketknife. I'm sure you know him. He spoke of you."

Endora listened, still as a statue.

"Anyway, the black's on my face so Zimboza, the Crag Lurcher, could recognize me. I'm the one who can break the Nesterclop's curse."

Endora squinted.

Dorothy reached into the knapsack and pulled out two drumsticks.

"Want one? They're really tasty," she said and extended one toward Endora while taking a bite out of the other.

With marked caution Endora walked closer, using the spear like a walking staff. She stopped within a few feet of Dorothy. She let go of her knife and inched her hand toward the chicken leg.

When the drumstick was just beyond her fingertips, she thrust her hand forward and snatched it from Dorothy's hand.

"You have pretty green eyes, Endora. Mine are green too. You see, we have something in common already."

Endora bit a large piece of meat off the drumstick and began chewing ferociously.

"Here, would you like some more?" Dorothy pulled another one from the bag.

Endora cleaned the remaining meat from the chicken leg with her next bite and tossed the bone into the fire. She reached for the second drumstick, this time with more civility. With one jaw bulging with chicken, she cracked a smile and nodded enthusiastically.

"Here. Want some water?" Dorothy reached down for the jug of water. She lifted it up to Endora. The feral woman dropped the spear and grabbed the jug. She turned it up and gulped, water running down from the edges of her mouth and onto her garment. Dorothy looked on as Endora lowered the jug to the ground and started ravaging the next chicken leg.

"Do you like cornbread?"

"Uh huh," Endora responded, her raised eyebrows displaying her eagerness.

Dorothy retrieved a large piece from the satchel and gave it to her. The strange woman shoved it into her mouth and bit off a chunk. She closed her eyes as if in ecstasy while she savored it.

"Have a seat." Dorothy said.

Endora accepted her invitation and sat down on the log. She cleaned the rest of the meat off the second drumstick, threw the bone into the flames and gobbled another piece of the cornbread. She picked up the jug and guzzled down more water. Dorothy reached into the knapsack and pulled out four cookies plus the un-eaten portion the boy had left. Dorothy kept one and the boy's leftover and offered the three remaining cookies to Endora.

"Mm! Mm!" Endora replied. She sat the water back down and took the cookies from Dorothy.

"Wow! These are really good, Endora," Dorothy said as she munched. "Don't you think?"

The mute woman looked at her with wide eyes and nodded with delight. Dorothy watched as Endora finished off the cornbread and wolfed down the cookies. The mysterious woman of Nimrod's Swamp didn't seem menacing or dangerous after all. If anything, she seemed skittish, even pitiful. Out of place. Struggling to survive. Not the malevolent, tongue-eating enchantress Dorothy had heard about. What was Endora's story? And, how did she come to have such a notorious reputation? Why did the mention of her name strike fear in those who heard it?

"Endora, is it true that you can write?"

The question startled Endora. Her eyes shot open. She stopped chewing and looked around. She turned to Dorothy and brought an index finger to her lips.

"Mm. Mm," she groaned.

"Don't tell anybody? Is that what you're trying to say?"

Endora nodded in affirmation and crossed her heart.

"Okay. I won't tell. I promise. But, why is it a secret?"

Endora stood up and looked around again.

"What's wrong?"

Endora raised an open palm to communicate. *Wait*. She walked away from the fire a bit and peered into the darkness.

"What are you looking for? Is something out there?"

Endora waved a hand up and down encouraging Dorothy to be quiet. Dorothy watched as Endora walked around, staring into the night. After navigating around the campfire a couple of times, she returned to the log she'd been sitting on. She picked up a stick and scrawled on the ground: *He doesn't know I write*. She looked at Dorothy and then rubbed the words out with her foot.

"Who?"

Endora wrote the letter "N" in the dirt, then drug her foot over it.

"N?" Dorothy tightened her lips and pondered. "N . . . you mean the Nesterclop?"

Endora nodded. Dorothy thought for a moment. Then, it occurred to her.

"Well, if the Nesterclop doesn't know you can write, then he doesn't know that you revealed the curse's secret to Zimboza."

Linmar burst from Dorothy's pocket and up to her shoulder.

"Eee! Eee!" he squeaked and flicked his tiny tail like a whip.

Endora looked with confusion at Linmar.

"This is Linmar. He's my special friend."

Dorothy brought an open hand to Linmar. The chipmunk climbed inside, squeaking and flipping his tail in heightened excitement.

"Oh, it's okay, Linmar. Endora's our friend. Right, Endora?"

Endora nodded.

"See, Linmar. I told you. Now, back you go." She returned the chipmunk to her dress pocket.

"Now, as I was saying. Since the Nesterclop doesn't know you can write. He can't know that you revealed the curse's secret to Zimboza. Which means he can't know that I really can break the curse."

"I do now!" came a voice from behind Dorothy and Endora.

Dorothy jumped to her feet and turned.

The Nesterclop strolled from the dimness into the light of the campfire.

Endora shoulders slumped. She rocked back and forth in a nervous fright.

The Nesterclop clutched the lapels of his tuxedo jacket and walked closer to Dorothy. "So, Dorothy. We meet again."

Dorothy leered at him, one side of her top lip raised.

The Nesterclop began pacing in front of her. "I underestimated you. I must admit. The idea that a young girl from some land called Kansas could come to my land and break my curse seemed to me . . .," he rolled his hand in the air a few times. "Should I say . . . outlandish in the least. But, now that I know what Endora's been keeping from me, it does all make sense. The Devil's Spit on your face. You rescuing the Hunchback and returning his mountain back to him." He raised an index finger and moved it left and right. "There's still no water by the way. And won't be as long as I have a say." He clutched the lapels of his jacket again. "I assume you've come here to complete the second task of the curse's secret: To show love to the unlovely."

The Nesterclop walked over and touched Endora on the shoulder. "And, she is indeed unlovely."

He stooped down and looked at her. "Why, you are the most hideous creature in all the land of the Red Brick Road. Altogether hideous I might add. Not even your own offspring could love you. If you had an offspring."

Dorothy jumped to her feet. "You shut up! You devil, you! She's a nice person! And, pretty too! I bet if someone combed her hair and gave her nice things to wear, she'd be as beautiful as any princess in the land."

"You think so, do you?"

"I most certainly do."

With wet eyes and a smile, Endora looked up at Dorothy.

The Nesterclop stood up. "Now that's noble and kind of you, Dorothy."

He put a hand on his chest. "And, such words would touch my heart . . . if I had one. But lest we waste valuable time . . . ," He made a backhanded wave. "Let me show you the side of Endora you've been hearing about."

He turned to Endora. "Get up!"

Endora stood up as if jerked by an invisible rope from above.

"Mm. Mm," she groaned, shaking her head in protest and backing away from the campfire. The Nesterclop pulled a gold chain from inside the front of his jacket. At the end of it a chain dangled a locket. Endora began to wail. The Nesterclop gazed at Endora and started swinging the locket like a pendulum.

"Needle prick. Candle wick," he said.

Endora stopped, closed her eyes and lowered her head. She took a deep breath and exhaled, then raised her head again. Her eyes shot open. No longer were they beautiful and green. Now they were pitch black. She peered at Dorothy and grinned, revealing dark, jagged, gruesome teeth.

Dorothy jumped back in horror. Endora rushed to Dorothy and grabbed her by the neck with one hand, forcing her to the ground. She pulled the knife from her belt and tightened her grip on Dorothy's throat. With Dorothy gagging underneath her, Endora let out an eerie squeal and lowered the blade of the knife to Dorothy's mouth. Dorothy fought to keep the blade from touching her.

The Nesterclop sashayed over. He stood over Dorothy and looked down, swinging the locket. "You know, Dorothy, I have a sneaking suspicion that you, my spirited little she-ling, are destined for fame. I envision some future author taking up his pen and writing of your very soon-to-be misfortune at the hands of Endora."

The Nesterclop squatted down and peered at her. "Think about the story line, Dorothy." He stretched an imaginary headline into the night air. "*A fiendish witch cuts out and eats the only tongue that ever defended and complimented her.* He made a fist and shook his head. "I tell you, it will make for CLASSIC literature."

As if a giant spotlight was suddenly switched on, the place around the campfire became like daytime. The Nesterclop looked up and Endora sprang to her feet. The boy stood before them, the Sword of Jerubaal gleaming in his hand, his eyelids narrowed. "You shall cease and yield!" He walked closer.

The Nesterclop stood up slowly, his hands raised as if surrendering. Dorothy stood to her feet. Endora dropped to her knees, her chin touching her chest.

"This is now the second time I've rendered you powerless with regards to Dorothy. You know the decree of the Great-Hearted King. Do you not?" the boy said and held the end of the blade close to the Nesterclop's throat.

"Yes. I'm well acquainted with his decree."

"Then I suggest you leave this land."

"Very well. I shall be on my way." The Nesterclop returned the locket to the inside of his lapel and adjusted the knot of his necktie. "I've been itching to see the land of the Green Brick Road anyway. I understand it presents many opportunities for an enterpriser such as myself."

The Nesterclop tipped his top hat to the boy and Dorothy, then turned and walked away, whistling as he went. The Sword of Jerubaal dimmed. The Nesterclop disappeared into the darkness.

"What was all that about?" Dorothy asked. "You know, the decree of the Great-Hearted King and the second time and all?"

"The King has declared that, if ever the Nesterclop is forced into submission three times at the point of the Sword of Jerubaal, upon the third he shall be doomed to the bottom of the black lake forever."

Dorothy raised her hands, her palms turned upward. "Then, why doesn't the Great-Hearted King just come back and rid all the Land of Oz of the Nesterclop? You heard what he said. He's going to the land of the Green Brick Road. He'll do terrible things there just like he's done here."

The boy rested the sword on one shoulder. "It is foolish to question The Great-Hearted King. He and his ways can be mysterious and perplexing, but never proven imperfect. At the present he alone knows his reasons for his doings and his delays. When he returns, and return he will, all the answers to such questions will be made manifest. Until then, we must persevere in hope. Be encouraged. For the Great Hearted-King's decree has sent the Nesterclop from our parcel of Oz. No one in the land of the Red Brick Road will ever encounter him again."

"That's great!" Dorothy said. She began to pace about, a wide grin on her face. "So that must mean that his curse has come to an end. We should see water flowing any moment now. Every Crag Lurcher will have round eyes. Benellus will be free. And the honeybees will return to the woods near the gorge. And I . . . I shall have Toto back and be on my way to see the Wizard."

"I'm afraid that's not the case," said the boy. "For sure, the Nesterclop has left here never to return, but the power of his curse remains. And, I must tell you that the bloom of the dogwood branch now has but one petal remaining. You must be about your mission and I must be about other matters."

And, with that, the boy turned and took to the road.

Dorothy watched him as he walked away.

"Well, what do you think about that, Endora. No more Nesterclop. Not around here at least."

Dorothy turned around expecting to see a joyful Endora. Instead, the strange woman remained on her knees, her head down. She picked up a stick and wrote on the ground: "I'm sorry."

"It's okay. It wasn't your fault. The Nesterclop made you do it."

"I was going to kill you," Endora scribbled and looked up at Dorothy with a look of shame.

"But you didn't. Don't you see? Besides, I know that wasn't really you. Now, was it?"

"No," she wrote in the dirt.

"It's done and done. No need to think about it anymore. Now, take your seat. I want to show you something."

Endora rose from her knees and sat down on one of the logs. Dorothy reached for the knapsack and took out the brush and mirror.

"Here. You hold this," Dorothy handed her the mirror.

Endora held it as Dorothy brushed through the swamp woman's stringy, matted hair.

"See. Look how pretty you are."

Endora looked in the mirror and grinned as Dorothy continued making strokes with the brush. Dorothy gave Endora some options. Brushed to one side and hanging in front of one shoulder. A single ponytail. Parted evenly in the middle. Brushed straight back with all hair behind the shoulders. All hair up on the head.

"Hey, I have an idea." Dorothy took off the slippers. "Let's see if these fit you."

Dorothy knelt down at Endora's feet. She held one slipper out. Endora slid a foot inside. Dorothy held out the other and Endora slipped in her other foot.

"Just look at them, Endora. They look as if they were made for you."

Endora giggled and raised both feet off the ground. She moved them back and forth and watched the slippers sparkle in the light of the campfire.

"Go ahead. Give'em a try," said Dorothy and motioned with her hand for Endora to walk.

Endora stood up and walked back and forth in front of Dorothy a couple of times, a wide smile on her face. She sat back down on the log and proceeded to take off the first shoe. Dorothy reached out and gripped Endora's feet, ensuring that they stayed in the slippers.

"They're yours, Endora. I want you to have them."

Endora shook her head, protesting with humility.

Dorothy sliced her hand through the air. "I won't take no for an answer."

She felt confident and free to be chatty with the feared woman.

"I can be mighty headstrong when I want to be. Trust me. Besides, I have another pair of shoes anyway. These are a gift from me to you. I know you won't be able to wear them much out here in this swamp. But, now that the Nesterclop's gone, you can venture out into the towns and villages so everyone can get to know the real Endora. The one I know. These slippers will come in handy when you're walking on the Red Brick Road. Especially when the sun's in its full strength. Not to mention the effect they'll have on folk when they see you wearing them. They'll know you're not all mean and dangerous like the rumors they've heard. I bet you'll have lots of friends in no time."

Dorothy stood up and pulled the leather mocassins from her pocket. This aroused Linmar and he climbed to her shoulder. Dorothy pulled on the soft leather shoes.

"I'd love to stay longer, but I have to be going. I've got one more thing to do in order for the Nesterclop's curse to be broken. But you already know that don't you?"

Endora nodded.

"If I don't succeed before the last petal of the dogwood blossom falls, the Narrow-Eyes will awake from the Guardian Owl's sleeping spell. If they do, who knows what they'll do to Nargoul, Houstess and Harlice and all the other Round-eyes. I've enjoyed getting to know you and I sure hope we meet again."

Dorothy turned and started on her journey. Unbeknownst to her, more of the Devil's Spit had just vanished from her face. Now, there was only one thing left to do. Amend a transgression. And, she knew exactly which one was highest on the list. What she didn't know, however, was how she'd get to the one she'd so grievously transgressed against.

Chapter Seventeen

Dorothy walked along to the concert of bone-chilling creature sounds that screeched and echoed from deep within the murky woods of Nimrod's Swamp. Up ahead, the road came to an abrupt dead end. And, there . . . there it stood.

The great barrier.

The one undone thing that hindered Dorothy from completing the third and final task of her mission, from breaking the Nesterclop's curse.

She stepped up and probed the obstruction's surface with an opened hand. Rough. Solid. Impenetrable. Once, it had been a means of travel. A mystical capsule that transported her from Decision Depot to the land of the Red Brick Road. Now, it was a broad, tall, mass of living wood reaching high into the starless sky. Dorothy took a few steps back and gazed up at the boughs and leafy branches. Linmar crouched on his hind legs, his warm, furry body touching Dorothy's neck.

"I wish you could talk," Dorothy said to Linmar. "I could sure use some advice right about now. There's gotta be a way to make this tree turn back into the elevator. Some special words. A special knock. A special branch to pull on. Something. We have to get back to Decision Depot."

The firm tap on Dorothy's shoulder startled her. She gasped as she jerked in reflex and turned on her heels. Endora stood before her holding up the slippers. She grunted and gave a *go ahead, take them* nod. Dorothy took a deep breath, a hand to her chest.

"You bout scared me to death, Endora."

Endora continued to hold up the slippers, her expression unchanged by Dorothy's comment.

"No. They're yours," Dorothy said. "Remember? I gave them to you."

Endora shook her head and rapped the side of the tree with the end of her spear. She held the slippers close to Dorothy's face, juddering them and grunting loudly.

"The slippers? The slippers will transform the tree into an elevator again?"

"Mm. Mm," Endora responded with a smile and excited eyes.

"Well, okay. If you say so."

Dorothy took the enchanting shoes. "Here. We'll trade then." She removed the mocassins from her feet and offered them to her.

Endora concurred and took them. Dorothy slid her feet into the slippers and turned around. She anticipated seeing an elevator door. To her confusion, the tree remained.

Dorothy looked back at Endora. "So, what now?"

Endora stepped up next to Dorothy and pointed to her own feet. Dorothy looked down. Endora touched her heels together three times then gave Dorothy an elbow nudge.

"Oh, so I have to do that, huh?"

Dorothy touched the heels of the sparkling shoes together once . . . twice . . . three times. The great tree vibrated. Each leaf transformed into a spoonful of light and took flight from the branches like a swarm of fireflies. Like an umbrella blown inside out by the wind, the barren limbs turned upward.

Dorothy stepped back.

The tree's trunk and branches fused together as if made of clay and stretched into the dark sky and beyond the clouds. Golden liquid burst from the cracks in the rough bark, rippling over the bark and hardening into solid, shiny metal. The outline of a door appeared. Like a formation of charging soldiers, the lights raced down from the sky. Starting just above the door, the lights began attaching themselves in perfect lines on the gleaming structure. Dorothy peered upward as the lights climbed into the heavens, row by row, along the side of the elevator. With the crisp ring of a bell, the door glided open.

"It worked, Endora! It worked!" Dorothy turned and hugged Endora. "Oh, thank you! Thank you!"

Endora broke from Dorothy's embrace, waving her hand toward the open door, grunting.

"Yes, yes, I must be going. After all, I have only one dogwood blossom left."

Dorothy hurried through the elevator door. She spun around, expecting to see Endora. Endora wasn't there.

Dorothy surveyed the several multi-colored buttons inside the compartment and pressed the one that was twice the size of all the others. The large letters "DD" lit up and the door closed. Dorothy's stomach fluttered as the elevator car rocketed upward.

She hoped the line would be short. If it wasn't, she'd wait her turn this time.

The elevator slowed and came to a stop. Ding. The door opened. Dorothy stepped out into the spacious room. No line of travelers. No announcements over the loud speakers. No one offering directions and assistance. The place was silent. Empty.

The tap of each step reverberated off the walls as Dorothy walked across the hard floor to the door—his door. Oh, how she hoped that he'd prove to be as forgiving as he was wise. That he'd see the sincerity of her apology. That he'd discern that she'd changed. Really changed.

"Okay, Linmar. Here I go."

Dorothy took a deep breath and reached for the handle. She tried it. Wouldn't budge. A second time with a firmer grip and more ratcheted force. Nothing doing. She sighed and slumped her shoulders.

Locked.

Her ever-faithful little friend held his position on her shoulder and sniffed the air inside the dim, hollow room. Dorothy released the doorknob and turned around slowly. She leaned back against the door. Linmar scurried down her arm and jumped to the floor.

"Where are you going?"

Her words bounced off the paneled walls.

Linmar darted across the floor to a row of back-to-back benches. He leaped to the side of one of them and hustled up it. Without hesitating, he bolted across its top and stopped close to the wall.

"*Eek! Eek!*" he squealed, standing on his back legs, looking at Dorothy.

"What's over there?"

She ran over to see.

A familiar figure lay on the bench, his hands folded over his stomach. His belly swelled and retracted with each silent breath he took. A blue hat was pulled down over his face, the tips of his orange mustache sticking out from the sides of the brim.

Dorothy squatted down and gave him a few good pokes. "Mister! Mister!"

The man mumbled and moved but settled back into to his deep sleep.

Dorothy started shaking the man by his shoulders. "Mister! Please wake up! I need your help!"

The lethargic sleeper shifted and wrestled to gain alertness. He pushed his hat up on his head, raised himself up half way and propped on one elbow. After a big yawn, he rubbed his eyes and sat up on the bench.

He looked at Dorothy through half-closed eyelids. "Is it morning already?"

"I'm Dorothy from Kansas. Remember me?"

He rubbed his eyes again and stroked the whiskers above his top lip. "I remember. How could I EVER forget you?" He rolled his eyes. "For that matter, how could anyone forget you?"

The man pulled his pocket watch from his inside his vest and studied it. He drew down his brow. "Don't tell me this thing has quit."

He held it up to one ear.

"Naw, it's working." He checked the time again. "Still have five more hours. No need to get up yet."

The man looked up at Dorothy. "How did you get in here anyway?"

"The elevator brought me here from the Red Brick Road. I need to talk to the Wearer of the White Crown."

The man pulled back his head. "You've come here from the Red Brick Road, you say?"

"Yes. I'm on—"

"Nobody travels on the Red Brick Road anymore," the man interrupted. "Folks say it's cursed."

"It is but I'm on a mission to break it. That's why I'm here. I need to see the Wearer of the White Crown. ASAP."

"I hate to disappoint you, but he's not here. So, you might as well save all your demanding and insisting and ASAP-ing for another day."

"When will he be?"

The man returned the watch back to his vest pocket. "Tomorrow."

The word stabbed Dorothy's heart.

She tightened her face. "But you don't understand!" Desperation began climbing up from her gut and gnawing at her throat. "I just have to see him! I just have to!"

The man huffed and shook his head. "Yep, just as I remember. Selfish up one side and bullheaded down the other."

Dorothy fanned her hands. "No, no! It's not like that at all. I'm not asking to see him for my sake, but for all those who live in the land of the Red Brick Road. The land is under a curse just like you've heard. I can help them. I can break the curse, but in order to do so, I have to see the Wearer of the White Crown."

"Sorry, but it ain't gonna happen. Not today anyway. Today's a high holiday. Hopscotch Day. The first day after a triple-colored moon. It's the one day when every citizen in these parts, including the Wearer of the White Crown, is allowed and expected to take a break from everything and sleep the entire day. So, you might as well find you a place to lay down and start performing your civic responsibility like all the rest of us."

The man laid back down on the bench. He pulled his hat back down over his eyes and folded his hands over his belly.

Dorothy tapped the man on one shoulder. "No, no! Please don't go back to sleep! Please help me!"

She shook him with both hands. "I have to see him before the last petal falls from the dogwood blossom or the curse will remain! Please! Please! At least tell me where he lives!"

The man breathed in and out deep breaths, sleeping a stubborn sleep as if under the power of a drug.

Dorothy sat down on the floor. She folded her arms on the top of her knees and rested her head.

She'd failed.

Tears overflowed her eyes and ran down her face, dropping onto her dress. She considered the future of those she'd met as she wailed. The water from the Hunchback's mountain would never flow again. The great flowers wouldn't grow again. No honey. No gillyberries. The Crag Lurchers would be forever at odds with each other. The Round-Eyes would remain enslaved to the Narrow-Eyes. And, Nargoul, Houstess and Harlice—what would Monguzi and Egscar do to them?

No. She couldn't just stand by and let this happen.

She might not be able to break the curse, but she could do the next best thing—free the Round-eyes from slavery and rescue Benellus from the Prison of Keylon. She didn't need magic; she had her friends, and she had herself.

Dorothy reached toward Linmar. The chipmunk jumped onto the back of her hand and scampered up her arm.

Dorothy hurried over and stepped inside the opened door. She pushed the red button. The door closed and the elevator descended.

It slowed its descent and stopped with a jolt. The door slid open.

Chapter Eighteen

The dim early morning still awaited the appearance of the morning sun. Thick moss hung from tree branches and dangled over the road like the shrouds of an army of grim reapers. Dorothy exited and walked with resolve on her trek for the dry riverbed. As she rounded the bend, she noticed what looked to be someone leaning against one of the trees along the edge of the road.

Was it him? Or was a creature she never met before. Friendly? She hoped so. Deadly? She prayed not.

She walked closer, her eyes fixed on the silhouette. It made a routine, predictable motion. It held its position, undeterred by the gentle tapping sound of the slippers against the bricks.

Could it be him? Could it really be him?"

The figure made a sound . . . a familiar sound. It was him.

Dorothy broke into a trot, the shoes clicking on the hard surface of the road. As she drew near to him he didn't look up at her. He just continued to cut slithers out of the chunk of wood.

Dorothy stopped near to him. "Oh, I'm so glad to see you," she said, holding her sides, breathing heavily.

The boy stopped his whittling and inspected his work. He looked up at her and cracked a smile. "Well, well, well. If it ain't the great curse-breaker from the land of Kansas!"

Dorothy shook her head. "I'm no great curse-breaker. I've failed. I can't complete the third part of the mission."

"So, what are you going to do now?"

Dorothy took in deep breaths of air. Her heart rate eased closer to normal. "I'm going back to the dry river bed to free the Round-eyes from the Narrow-eyes."

"You and the Round-eyes are no match for the Narrow-eyes."

"I know. I was hoping you'd come too."

The boy pressed his lips together and drew down his brow.

"Please say you'll help me. The Round-eyes are good and deserve to be free."

"I don't disagree with you on that."

"Then you'll help?"

The boy stood, folded his knife shut and shoved it into his pocket along with the piece of wood. "And, what if I say no?"

Dorothy gave him a cool expression. "Then I'll go without you."

He raked a hand through his hair as he walked to the edge of the road.

"It'll be dangerous," he said, gazing into the fog-dressed trees of the swamp.

Dorothy walked up next to him. "I don't doubt that," she said. "But I won't let it stop me."

The boy pulled a twig from a tree and chewed the end of it. "Why would you risk your neck for a bunch of Round-eyes anyway?"

"They can't free themselves."

The boy turned and looked at her through tight eyelids. "No, they can't. Is that the only reason?"

Dorothy folded her hands and tilted her head. "They risked theirs for me. I owe them. Besides, they're my friends. You helping or not? I need to get going. It's a long way."

The boy tossed the twig, gave her a half wink and smiled. "I know a shortcut." He motioned with his head. "Let's get going."

He started walking. Dorothy walked beside him.

She looked up at him as they went along. "How's Toto doing?"

"He's fine," the boy said, keeping his attention on the way ahead.

"I sure hope he's being taken good care of." Dorothy cut a look at the boy's profile. "Is he being given plenty to eat?"

The boy kept walking, gazing ahead. "No need to worry about him. He's fine. Eating like a prince."

"I miss him something terrible. I'm sure he misses me too. Probably whimpers and yelps all through the night wanting me to be next to him."

"You think so?"

"Oh, I'm sure of it. I bet when he sees me again, he'll bark and come running. He'll jump right up into my arms and lick me all over my face."

"I don't think he really misses you, Dorothy," the boy said. He looked at her, one of his eyebrows raised. "I saw him just the other day and he looked pretty happy to me."

Dorothy swallowed hard. "That's because he's a very brave and resilient dog. He once stood down a bobcat in the barn all by himself until Uncle Henry could come with his rifle."

The boy didn't acknowledge her words. He just kept walking.

They came to the bottom of a slight hill.

The boy veered off the road. He pushed some of the thick, low hanging moss to one side and looked back at Dorothy. "Okay, this way. Pay attention and watch where you step till we get out of this swamp. This place is crawling with red diamond vipers. If one bites you, you'll be dead before I can get you to a doctor."

The boy stepped into the swamp. Dorothy slipped through as he'd done, following behind him. Did Toto really not miss her? She pushed a branch aside, but it whipped back and hit her in the face. "Ow!"

The boy stopped and looked back at her, smirking. "If you'd focus and stop thinking about your dog—"

"I'm not thinking about my dog!" Her voice came out louder than she'd meant it to.

"Pick it up and stay close. We need to get to high ground. I don't have my lantern to ward off the Clutchboggins."

"What are Clutchboggins?"

"They lurk behind the trees. If they capture you, you have to bargain with them before they'll turn you loose."

"Bargain for what?"

"Anything they might want for their clutch."

Dorothy drew down her brow and raised one side of her mouth. "Their clutch?"

"The secret place where they keep their treasures. Clutchboggins horde things. All kinds of things. They're never satisfied with what they have."

The boy paused and pointed to a leafy plant he'd just walked past. "Be careful not to rub up against that," he said. "It'll make you itch for two days."

He watched as Dorothy took deliberate steps. When she was clear of the odious plant he resumed the trudge through the marsh.

"Clutchboggins sound like horrid creatures," Dorothy said.

The boy broke a low-hanging branch to clear the way. "They're not as bad as Scaithes or Treetrolls, but better off avoided nonetheless."

He stepped over a fallen tree then turned back to her. He reached out and took her hand. His grip was firm, his hand warm . . . she liked it. As she raised her foot to hurdle the obstruction, he lifted her. She cleared the tree trunk without effort as the boy carefully hoisted her over it. He was strong.

"If you come across a Clutchboggin," the boy continued. "You want to keep anything valuable out of their sight. If they see something they want, they'll grab it with one of their four hands before quick can get ready."

"A Clutchboggin has four hands?"

"Yes," the boy said and leaped across a mud bog to a dry patch of soil. The ground under his feet made a cracking sound as if he'd broken a stick. A bent over tree snapped upright, pulling a rope taut. The noose at the end tightened around the boy's ankles and the rope snatched him upward. In an instant, the boy hung in the air, suspended by his feet. The pocketknife and block of wood fell out of his pocket and landed on the ground underneath him.

"*Ayeee!*" Dorothy screamed.

The commotion stirred Linmar from his nap. He bolted out of Dorothy's pocket and climbed to her shoulder.

"Well," the boy said, his shirt hanging down over his face. "This is what I get for not paying better attention!"

He shook his head and exhaled then pulled himself up and began trying to reach the rope that bound his ankles. The rope swung and spun as he labored.

"It's a Clutchboggin booby trap!" he said. "Quick! Help me get down!"

"Your knife!" Dorothy shouted back and jumped over the bog.

She reached down and picked up the pocketknife. "Here, I'll open it for you," she said and pulled open the shiny blade.

The boy reached out his hand to take the knife.

Before Dorothy and the boy could make the exchange, a hairy, beefy-fingered hand shot between them, fisted the knife and stole it away.

"I'll be taking this!" a nasally voice said.

Dorothy jumped back in fright. She turned. An ape-like creature stood before her. In one of his four hands he held the pocketknife.

The creature's kindred accomplice strolled over to the dangling boy. "The shortcut to the dry river bottom never disappoints," he said. He walked around the boy, looking him up and down. "This makes four captures in five days. What do you think this is, Baltar?"

"Looks to be some type of small, folding sword," Baltar said, working the blade of the knife, closing and opening it.

"I don't mean that do-lolly of a thing. I mean this prisoner."

Baltar continued to focus on the pocketknife. He folded it close and tucked it under one of his leather wristbands. "Look. I could conceal it and no one would ever know I had it. Could be useful when we're thieving. I could walk right up to someone then___" He jerked the knife back out and opened it. "I could draw it like this and demand all his curios and coins."

Baltar came close to the boy and held the knife up in front of the boy's face. "I've never seen anything like this. I desire it most intensely. Let me keep it and I'll spare your life."

"The answer is no!" the boy shot back. "No deal!"

"So, you won't part with it even for your own freedom?"

The boy looked up, his expression stern as if he were ready to fight. "Not on your life!"

Baltar took a few steps away from the boy. He opened and closed the knife a few more times. "That must mean it's a very special sword." He looked back at the boy. "Does it have magic in it?"

The boy closed his eyes and sighed.

For the first time, Dorothy paid attention to the details of the knife. Baltar held it up and turned it over several times, inspecting it as it glistened in the sunrays that speared down through the tree foliage above. He studied the knife's polished black onyx handle.

"It's magnificent," he said. "A white crown on one side and a white owl on the other. Remarkable workmanship."

He held it up for his partner to see. "Have you ever seen anything like it?"

The other Clutchboggin grabbed the boy by his chin and forced his mouth open. "Odd. He has smooth teeth. Must eat berries and nuts and such. I'd have guessed him to be a meat eater."

The boy slapped the Clutchboggin's hand away.

"Look, Saltooth. It even has a second, smaller blade," Baltar said, holding up the knife with both its blades opened.

Saltooth grunted, gave the boy a shove and looked at Baltar. "Let's keep the sword and leave him hanging here. He won't last long. The Treetrolls will have his carcass picked clean by morning."

Baltar clutched the casing of the knife in a fist, the blades sticking out on each side of his hand. He whipped his fist in the air a few times as if he were fighting with an opponent. "We're not leaving him for the Treetrolls. He's far too valuable. Besides, what have Treetrolls ever done for us? Just look how young and strong he looks. He has many years ahead of him. He'll make a superb Molewiggin slave. I bet they'll give a sizable gem for him."

The boy threw Baltar a contemptuous look. "Do whatever you want. I'm not giving it to you."

"Very well," Baltar said. "Saltooth, bind him and let him down."

Baltar closed the blades and re-tucked the knife under the leather band.

Saltooth tied the boy's hands behind his back then slipped the noose of a rope over the boy's head and secured it around his neck. He held the end of the rope and released the tension on the booby trap, lowering the boy to the ground. "Get up!" he commanded. The boy stood up. Saltooth reached down and picked up the block of wood that had fallen out the boy's pocket. "Why do you think he had this in his pocket?"

Baltar glanced at it. "Who knows? Looks useless. Piece of a stump or something."

Saltooth gave the chunk another look then tossed it on the marshy ground. He raised two of his hands toward Dorothy. "And, what about her?"

"Just leave her. Who'd give anything for such a scrawny weakling. I have no use for her. Not even for her shiny shoes."

Saltooth shrugged his shoulders. "Okay. If you say so."

"Let's go," Baltar said. "I understand there's a clan of Singing-genies traveling on the road tonight. No telling what they'll be carrying in their caps and bonnets."

Dorothy watched as the Clutchboggins began making their way toward the Red Brick Road, the boy following at the end of the rope like a dog on a leash. She didn't understand the boy's impenetrable affinity for the pocketknife. Each boy she knew back in Kansas had more than a few such knives. They traded them. Sold them. Some even gave them away. She knew the cunning boy must have a reason for his unwillingness to relinquish it. She'd do all she could to help gain his freedom and get it back. Though she no longer was the Dorothy she used to be, she felt it appropriate, given the situation, to utilize some of her former spidery tactics.

"If a deal is what you desire, you'd do well to hear mine," she said.

The boy looked back to her. "Dorothy, don't deal with them! They're not to be trusted!"

Baltar stopped and turned around.

Dorothy stared him in the eyes.

Baltar grinned, displaying his large even teeth, canines at each side. "All . . . rrright! Maybe I sold you short." He walked back to her.

Saltooth stood and watched, holding the rope. The boy shook his head, then shot Dorothy a *what are you thinking* look.

"Okay! What do you have to trade?" Baltar said and interlocked the fingers of his two top hands.

Dorothy cocked her head back. "Name something you don't have. I'll get it for you."

Baltar shot his eyes open. "Now that's a deal I can't refuse." He rubbed his chin. "Let me see." He looked at her and smiled. "How about one of those ticking time-tellers on a gold chain? I've been wanting one ever since I saw the Nesterclop's."

"A pocket watch? So, you want a pocket watch, huh? Won't be easy to come by, but I think I can get one."

"My, my, my. What a little dealmaker you are! I believe you've got a little swamp water in your veins."

Dorothy took a few steps toward him. "It'll take some time. Probably a day or so, but if I get you a pocket watch, you have to let my friend go free."

"You got yourself a deal."

Dorothy peaked her eyebrows and raised an index finger. "And give him his sword back."

"Ouuuu! I like your style. We have a lot in common, you and me. But I don't do two for one bartering unless I'm the one getting the two. No deal."

Dorothy stared into Baltar's eyes, her face tight. She lifted an opened hand. "Fine," she said. "Name something else then! I might be willing to go two for two."

Baltar crossed his four arms and cut a look at her. "The second item is far more hazardous to come by. In fact, it could cost you your life."

Dorothy smirked. "Try me!"

"You strike as fast as a red diamond viper. I wonder if you're as venomous."

Dorothy rolled her eyes. "Spare me the metaphorical comparisons. We're wasting time."

"Very well then, if you're so anxious to lose your life. A noxious, tongue-eating witch lives in this swamp. She doesn't talk."

"Yeah. I've heard of her."

"She doesn't have to slurp her soup from a cup or a bowl like all the rest of us because she has a silver spoon. You bring me the spoon and I'll give the boy his sword. You have till dusk tomorrow." Baltar unfolded his arms and turned his four palms up. "If you're not back by then, we move on."

Dorothy headed toward the Red Brick Road.

"If it hadn't taken you so long to spit it out I could have been on my way already," she said as she walked.

Baltar raised his voice. "And, don't forget the time-teller!"

Dorothy turned around and shot Baltar a condescending look as she back stepped. "I told you. It's called a pocket watch. And, I won't forget it. You just be standing here when I return."

"I will. Like a tombstone in a graveyard, my little serpent! Like a tombstone in a graveyard!"

Dorothy huffed and spun around.

Chapter Nineteen

Dorothy stood at the front of the massive tree and clicked the heels of the slippers together three times. Just like before, the tree transformed into the magical elevator. The bell dinged. The door slid open and Dorothy stepped inside. She pushed the large "DD" button and the elevator car rocketed upward. WHERE to get a pocket watch and a silver spoon—that was easy. Actually getting there? Now, that was the question.

The elevator slowed to a stop. The door glided open and the sounds of a multitude of loud, overlapping conversations filled the car. Hopscotch Day had come and gone. Decision Depot once again teemed with travelers of every sort, all en route to some destination within the Land of Oz. Dorothy stepped out and a young, excited couple stepped in. Each wore a big red ribbon with the words *Just Married* inscribed on it. Dorothy scanned the busy room. In the middle of the crowd, one figure stood head and shoulders above all others. He wore a blue uniform with a matching blue hat.

He'd be able to advise her.

She started in his direction, weaving her way through the crowd, careful to beg for pardons and be as cordial as she possibly could given the density inside the station. When she got within arm's reach of the man, she gave a firm tug on the tail of his jacket. The man turned and looked down at her.

"Excuse me, sir," she said with a loud but polite voice. "It's me again. Dorothy from Kansas. Could you please tell me how I might get back to Munchkinland?"

"A peculiar young traveler, you are. In all my days I've never—"

Dorothy interrupted. "I know. I've been a real test of your good nature, I'm sure, but I'd be truly grateful for your assistance."

The man pointed to the front door. "See the doorman. He's outside on the porch."

"Thank you." Dorothy started toward the front door. She took a few steps. A thought came to mind. Maybe it still wasn't too late. She turned back to the man.

"Sorry, sir. But I have one more question."

The man twitched his mustache. "And what might that be?"

"Is the Wearer of the White Crown in today?"

The man tightened his face and shook his head. "No. He hasn't been in for some time now. Not sure when he'll be back."

Dorothy's heart sank. It seemed that all hope was lost. The curse would not be broken.

"Okay. Thank you," she said, then proceeded once again to make her way to the door.

Just before she reached it, she heard a distressed young-sounding voice.

"Mommy! Mommy! I want my mommy!"

Dorothy looked down to see a little girl. The child was no taller than Dorothy's waist. "I want my mommy," the girl said, her eyes and cheeks wet with tears.

Dorothy stooped down and patted her on the head. "Oh, baby. Don't you worry. We'll find your mommy."

The little girl gazed at Dorothy, her lips poked out, her eyebrows pulled down.

Dorothy took her and stood. She looked around the room. In the far corner, halfway between the floor and ceiling, a short, familiar man stood on a rostrum—the announcer with the prominent front tooth and the raisin-like mole on his face.

He leaned in close to the microphone. "No wisdom line today, folks. So have your destination decisions made by the time you reach the elevator."

Maintaining a firm hold on the little girl like a good big sister, Dorothy navigated through the thick crowd. When she reached the announcer's platform, she looked up at him and yelled, "Sir, I have a lost little girl here!"

Dorothy's words, however, failed to rise above the loud chatter of the numerous busy travelers. The man kept his focus on the crowd and repeated his announcement. When he completed it, Dorothy lifted her voice in a second attempt to get his attention.

"Sir, we need your help!"

No success.

Linmar emerged from Dorothy's pocket and sprang to the floor. The keen chipmunk dashed to the wall, and like climbing the trunk of a tree, scrambled up to the platform. He scurried in circles around the announcer's feet, chattering and swishing his tail. The commotion caught the man's attention.

"Ugh!" he shouted and jumped back.

The microphone blasted the man's frightened response over the speaker system. In an instant, the noisy travelers ceased their shuffling and conversing and looked up to the announcer. Linmar bolted back down the wall.

Dorothy seized upon the moment of sudden silence. "Sir!"

The man regained his composure and looked down at Dorothy and the bewildered youngster.

"This little girl has lost her mommy," Dorothy said. "Would you please make an announcement?"

"Certainly!" He looked at the sniffling child. "What's your name, little lassie?"

"Lilly Belle."

The man cleared his throat. "May I have your attention, please. If Lilly Belle is your daughter, she's right here below my platform waiting for you."

The man looked back down at Dorothy just as she was returning Linmar to her pocket. He covered the microphone with one hand. "And, if you don't mind, would you please keep your pet rat with you at all times while you're here."

"Okay. But he's not a rat. He's a chipmunk. The most amazing chipmunk you ever saw."

"I'm sure he is. But, if it's all the same to you, see that he stays in your pocket to avoid any further chaos."

A young woman with golden blonde hair emerged from the throng of travelers.

She dropped to her knees and embraced the tearful tot. "Oh, Lilly Belle, I've been looking all over for you. From now on, stay close to me." She kissed the child and tightened her embrace.

"I will, mommy."

Looking down on the joyful reunion, the man made eye contact with Dorothy.

"Thank you," Dorothy mouthed.

The man returned a wink and a smile then began repeating his routine announcements.

Dorothy pulled away from the scene and maneuvered her way through the mass of travelers until she reached the door. She opened it and stepped onto the porch. The doorman was nowhere to be seen.

A man leaned against a pillar of the porch, the crook of his walking cane hanging over one wrist.

Dorothy stepped up to him. "Sir, do you know where the doorman is?"

"You just missed him. Left here about five minutes ago. Said his shift was over."

Dorothy's heart sank and a pain rose in her throat. "Oh no! I really needed to speak to him."

The man patted her on the shoulder. "Now, don't fret yourself, young lady. I'm sure he'll be here tomorrow."

"I can't wait till tomorrow. I need to get back to Munchkinland . . . as soon as I can. It's critical."

The man pulled his head back and squinted. "Munchkinland?"

"Yes. It's on the other side of Sparkleberry Bridge."

The man cocked his head and smiled. "Well, there you have it, then. Just go to this Sparkleberry Bridge you speak of and you should see Munchkinland."

Dorothy sighed and shook her head. "I wish it were that easy. The bridge disappeared when I crossed it and the river became as wide as an ocean."

The man stroked his chin. "I see. That would complicate things, wouldn't it?" He raised an index finger. "I tell you what. I have several hours before I have to be somewhere. I'd be glad to come along with you. Perhaps we could figure things out together. What do you say?"

"I'd be ever so appreciative."

The man lifted his walking cane from his wrist. "Very well." He tilted his head and motioned to the steps with an opened hand. "After you."

As they walked along the path, Dorothy recounted to the man her experiences in the land of the Red Brick Road. About Nargoul and Houstess and Harlice. About Sput and the Gnomes and how they all worked together to free the Hunchback. She told him about the Nesterclop's curse and about Endora. About the boy with the pocketknife and how he was being held captive by the Clutchboggins. The man listened, hanging on Dorothy's every word like a delighted grandfather listening to his grandchildren.

The path ended at a thin beach. The teal blue water reached into the horizon and joined with the sky.

The man looked right and left then peered into the distance. "A bridge used to be here and this ocean used to be a river you say?"

"Yes. The bridge had a glass bottom and reached over the Sparkleberry River."

He looked down at her. "Are you sure?"

"Positive. My dog, Toto, and I walked across it to get to the depot."

"Mm, I see. You say it disappeared?"

"Yes sir."

The man rubbed his chin and looked up into the sky. "Ah-ha," he said and tapped the end of his cane on the pathway. He gave her a big smile. "If the bridge disappeared there must be a way to make it re-appear."

"I know something that might work," Dorothy said.

The man lifted the cane and pointed it to the end of it toward the massive body of water. "Then, by all means, give it a go."

Dorothy grabbed the hem of her dress and pulled the bottom of it close to her legs. She raised the toe of one of the slippers. "These shoes are magic."

"You don't say."

"Yessir. I was in a situation once and they proved to be just the ticket. Watch this."

Dorothy clicked the heels of the slippers together three times.

Nothing.

Dorothy pressed her lips together and wrenched one side of her face. "Hm. I must not be doing it loud enough. This time I'll tap them hard."

Dorothy squared her shoulders, touched the toes of the shoes together and kept her heels wide apart. She took a deep breath and twisted on the balls of her feet, scissoring the heels of the slippers together. Each tap was loud enough for the man to hear. Once again, the vast expanse of water remained. Nothing changed. Dorothy rounded her shoulders and exhaled, an expression of despair on her face.

"I've failed again! First, I couldn't break the Nesterclop's curse and now I can't free the boy. The Round-eyes will remain slaves to the Narrow-eyes forever! And, on top of everything, I'll never see Toto again!"

Dorothy wailed. She turned and fell into the man's embrace.

"Now, now," consoled the man as he patted her on the back. "Some things require faith, you know. Why not give IT a try?"

Dorothy released the man and took a step back.

"What do you mean?"

"You know . . . faith." He thrust an index finger high into the air. "Acting in the darkness as though it were light. Seeing the unseen so that you might do what seems impossible."

"Are you a preacher?"

The man laughed. "That's the first time I've ever been asked that. Go ahead, take a step of faith."

"But how?"

The man stepped to the edge of the water. He jammed the end of the cane down into the dirt. "Faith begins where things are." He raised it toward the horizon. "And then goes in the direction of the way things need to be."

Dorothy stepped up next to him and looked out across the water. "Faith begins where things are and then goes in the direction of the way things need to be, huh?"

"That's right." The man winked and gave an affirming nod.

"Okay. If the bridge were here, I'd walk across it. But, it's not. That's the way things are. But the bridge needs to be here so, here goes." Dorothy placed one foot in the water.

The slipper sank into the miry, soft bottom, the water up to her ankle.

She looked back at the man and shook her head. "Faith isn't working either."

"Sometimes faith means both feet!" the man said.

Dorothy paused for a moment, then put her other foot in the water. The waterline on the horizon drew closer and Munchkinland came into focus as if a great invisible hand were painting it.

Dorothy watched, her eyes large, a broad grin on her face.

The shore of Munchkinland came closer. When it reached a distance of a stone's throw, a glass pathway began to extend from it. The pathway formed under Dorothy's feet, lifting her up out of the water. The slippers, now suddenly dry and clean, glistened as before. Rails appeared along the bottom of the bridge. Large flowers grew. Fish began to swim. The multicolored parrot flew down and perched on a low hanging tree limb.

Something made a plop in the water. Dorothy looked down. The beach-ball-sized bullfrog sat on a large stone, one eye magnified by his looking glass, his derby hat tilted perfectly in place.

"It worked! It worked! Faith really worked," Dorothy said and looked back to the man.

He, however, was no longer there.

Dorothy walked across the glass-bottom bridge. The fish frolicked in the water. Hummingbirds busied themselves in the flowers that grew on the rails.

"She's back. She's back," the parrot squawked.

Dorothy stepped off the bridge and onto the main street of Munchkinland. The constable sat on a bench in front of the barbershop, his face hidden behind the morning's edition of the Munchkinland Gazette. The clicking of the slippers interrupted his reading. He lowered his newspaper and peered over the top of it. He twitched his head. Closed and opened his eyes.

"Well, twinkle my stars," he said and folded the newspaper.

He dropped it on the bench and jumped to his feet.

"What brings you back to Munchkinland? I thought you'd be well on your way to see the Wizard of Oz by now."

He hustled up to her and walked alongside her.

"Well, I've had a change of plans, sheriff. It's a long story. If I had time to stay and visit, I'd tell you all about it. But right now I need to get to my house. It's still here, isn't it?"

"Oh, yes. It's sitting over there where it landed." He pointed further up the road. "In the same condition as when you arrived, too. But your condition seems to the contrary. Seems like the Red Brick Road has had a tendering effect on you."

"Yep. It's part of the long story I mentioned. I best be on my way."

She picked up her pace.

The constable stood in the middle of Main Street and watched Dorothy trek to her house. A Munchkin with a tall top hat and a pointed goatee kept his eyes on Dorothy as he walked up to the head lawman. "Is that who I think it is?"

"Not exactly," the constable said. "To the eye, she's who you think she is, but to the heart, she's seems to be someone else altogether."

· ·

Dorothy swung open the screen door. The broken tension spring allowed it to swing back and clap against the front of the house. She pushed on the main door and walked inside. The smell of Aunt Em, Uncle Henry and Kansas farmland greeted her. Furniture, pictures and dishes remained in place as if the tornado had gently sat the house down in Munchkinland. Dorothy entered Aunt Em and Uncle Henry's bedroom. She pulled open the top dresser drawer and searched through the humble man's accessories. Cuff links, army medals, tie tacks, two handkerchiefs with the initial "H" embroidered on them (neither of which had ever been used), round spectacles that wrapped around the ears, a money clip with a rooster on it, and finally, what Dorothy was looking for—a pocket watch. Uncle Henry had won it one year at the ring toss booth at the county fair. He'd aimed for the ivory pipe. He loved a good pipe late at night before bed. The ring, however, bounced off the pipe and looped around the pocket watch. Uncle Henry cared little for it. Never used it. The watch was nice. Had a second hand. But the kind old uncle had always said it was too uptown for him—a man who wore overalls everyday . . . even to church on Sundays. Dorothy was sure he wouldn't mind her taking it and certainly wouldn't miss it. She grabbed it and shut the drawer.

Dorothy exited the bedroom, walked to the pantry and pulled back the curtain. Shelves of canned goods lined one wall of the room. Dry goods filled the shelves on the opposite side. Near the back of the room, a chord hung from the ceiling. Dorothy reached for it, but paused before taking it in her hand. She took a deep breath, her conscience feeling as if a long, dry thorn were bearing into it. To get the silver spoon she'd have to go against the wishes of the one woman Dorothy knew truly loved her.

Aunt Em had filled the void left by the unknown woman who'd birthed and abandoned Dorothy. Henry and Emily never had children of their own. They couldn't. The first failed pregnancy of the early days of their marriage had made their home a childless one. That is, until Dorothy came to them many years later. Since that time, Aunt Em had doted over Dorothy and coddled her as elderlies tend to do. Dorothy had known but a few rules growing up and experienced only meager consequences when she violated them. Uncle Henry and Aunt Em could never find the courage to discipline her. Nonetheless, Aunt Em had one firm prohibition: the cedar trunk in the attic was strictly off limits. Dorothy knew it would be hers . . . one day. "It's your hope chest. It's for your wedding day and not before!" Aunt Em reminded Dorothy time and time again. She never allowed Dorothy in the attic unless she or Henry accompanied her. And, for extra measure, she had Henry install a bell at the top of the staircase leading up to it. She knew Dorothy to be a crafty girl. Try as she may, Dorothy could never contrive a way to lower the stairs without causing the bell to ding.

Though Dorothy had never seen the things inside the mysterious chest, she knew of a few of the items nonetheless. Not because Aunt Em had told her, but because Dorothy had often eavesdropped on Parson Claxton and Aunt Em's pastoral conversations. Ever so often the right reverend came for a visit that consisted of lunch followed by a sit down in the parlor. Each time he came he brought something wrapped in brown paper. Sometimes the package was small. Sometimes it was large. From time to time Dorothy would ask the minister about the package he'd brought that day. "It's just a little matter for your Aunt Em to tend to," he'd answer and then change the subject to his previous Sunday's sermon. On a day when he visited, later on that night, while Dorothy was in bed and supposed to be asleep, she'd hear the bell ding as Aunt Em would lower the staircase and climb to the attic. Dorothy would listen as the loving guardian walked over the ceiling to the intriguing chest, open it and add the pastor's package to the collection. Dorothy had counted eleven trips to the chest since Parson Claxton started bringing the packages. During one of her snooping sessions, she heard the pastor say silverware had arrived from Mississippi. And, later on that night, just as Dorothy suspected, she heard Aunt Em traipse over the ceiling of her bedroom and deposit the package in the cedar chest.

Dorothy recalled Parson Claxton's sermon on Rahab entitled "A Time to Lie." She could still picture in her mind the trusted minister standing behind his pulpit and, with piqued passion, extoling Rahab's virtue for lying to save the lives of the Israelite spies. "Sometimes you must violate a lesser commandment to keep a greater," he repeated throughout his oratory. Surely, this was one of those times. Dorothy hurdled the moral dilemma, grabbed the cord and lowered the staircase. The trusty bell dinged.

With Linmar looking out from the top of her dress pocket, Dorothy climbed the creaky steps. Like a spotlight, the sun's rays speared through the attic window and onto the trunk. Dorothy walked to it, counseling herself on the rightness of her decision. She knelt down and lifted the bulky wood lid. A white dress folded to perfection laid on top a large brown package, numerous smaller brown packages were stacked next to it. Dorothy began. She took out the first one. It was heavy, but small—too small to contain silverware. She sat it on the floor and reached for another. The next one was big enough. She shook it. No sound. Couldn't be silver. Dorothy continued inventorying the items until she came to a firm, heavy package.

"This might be what I'm looking for, Linmar."

She gave it a gentle shake. Metal objects clanged on the inside. Dorothy untied the string that wrapped around the package and removed the brown paper.

"Wow, this is beautiful!" Dorothy ran her fingers over the carving on top of the elegant wooden box. "It's an oak leaf."

Dorothy loosened the clasp and opened it. Rows of silver knives, forks, servers and spoons of different sizes lay inside the royal blue felt lining of the box. The handle of each utensil had an oak leaf etched on it matching the carving on the outside of the case.

"Aren't they magnificent, Linmar?"

She removed the pie server from the collection and inspected it, her heart pumping at the sight of the exquisite culinary tool as it gleamed in the sunlight.

Wait. This was no time to be captivated by luxuries. The boy was in danger. She had to get going. She returned the pie server to its place. Took out a soup spoon and shut the decorative case.

Dorothy stood and shoved the spoon into her pocket. As she started making her way back to the attic door, she stopped. What if the Wizard of Oz transported her back to Kansas in the house?

After all, it was the vehicle that had brought her to Munchkinland in the first place. So it stood to reason that it could be the vehicle to carry her back home. Best to leave the chest as she'd found it. Dorothy turned and hurried back to the chest. She re-wrapped the exquisite box with the brown paper and secured it once again with the string. Then, she re-stacked the packages inside the chest and closed it.

She hurried to the attic stairs and descended back down to the pantry. The bell dinged as she pushed the folded staircase up to the ceiling.

Now, to get through Decision Depot and back to the boy.

Chapter Twenty

Dorothy retraced her steps through the swamp, climbing over fallen trees, leaping over waterholes and navigating around marsh patches. The sound of heated, dissenting voices grew louder as she drew closer to the place where she'd left the boy with Baltar and Saltooth. Dorothy slowed her pace and took calculated, stealthy strides until she reached the edge of the captive spot. She positioned herself behind a tree and spied on the commotion. More than two dozen crusty, wrinkled creatures encircled the two Clutchboggins. Each had a crooked horn growing from the top of its forehead. Two eyes, one above the other and pointed, leathery ears.

One of the creatures held the end of the rope that was tied around the boy's neck. The boy appeared annoyed. Defiant. Dorothy smiled at the sight of him.

"I told you. She'll be back for the boy," Baltar said to the tallest of the creatures. "When she gets here, you can have them both. I have no use for them. Once she gives me the silver spoon, we'll be on our way. Do whatever you like with them. But, she's clever, I tell you. She's not gonna come into the camp if you and your clan are here holding us at knifepoint." He raised his spear and looked up into the tops of the trees. "Wait in the treetops if you like."

The tall one scanned his eyes upward, but made no reply. One of the creatures hobbled over to the boy and looked him up and down. He hacked up a mouth full of green slime and spat it on the ground then turned to the tall one. "The Clutchboggin might have a point," he said.

The tall one rolled his eyes and returned a repulsive look to his counterpart. "Did I ask for your counsel?"

The creature coughed and spat again. "No sir. I was just trying to help."

"No sir. I was just trying to help," the tall one repeated in a mocking voice, a contemptuous look on his face. He relaxed his expression. "Come here. Let me tell you something," he said.

The creature grinned, displaying his only three top teeth. He limped over to his superior.

The tall one put his arm around the minion's shoulders and began to walk with him. "Tell me if you think this is a good idea."

The congested one smiled in gitty enthusiasm. "Sure, sir. Tell me what do you have in mind?" The grin on his face turned to a grimace, however, when the tall one plunged his knife into his belly.

Dorothy gasped and brought her hand to her mouth. What a brutal beast.

The boy held his insolent composure.

The tall one gripped the underling by the back of the neck, clamped his teeth together and drove the knife in further. He jerked it out and the minion fell to the ground, gurgling.

The tall one stooped down, wiped the bloody blade on his dead companion's loincloth, returned his knife to its sheath then stood up. "Give the boy back to the Clutchboggins."

The creature that held the boy in custody obeyed without delay and handed the rope to Saltooth.

"I'll give you a half an hour," the tall one said to Baltar. "If she doesn't show, we'll know you're bluffing. And then we'll . . . well, I'll just let you wonder."

He looked at his partners. "Find you a limb, fellas, and let's wait and see if this talk about a crafty female is true."

The creatures sheathed their knives and shimmied up the trees with the ease of walking across a floor.

Dorothy faded back into the forest to avoid being seen by them. She'd wait to see how they'd deal with the two Clutchboggins when the half-hour was up. Then, she'd decide what to do to free the boy. He'd proven to be faithful, always there when she needed him most, always acting with a greater purpose, always doing what was best for her. Except for taking Toto. Dorothy was beginning to think, however, she'd come to see his wisdom even in doing THAT. Though she'd known the boy but for a short time, he'd had an indelible impact on her. Just as a gifted sculptor transforms a useless, lifeless rock into a desirable piece of art, the boy had transformed her. With his words and with his actions. Perplexing and hurtful as they were at times, they proved to be necessary and beneficial. Why he'd bothered himself with her,

Dorothy didn't know. What she did know, however, is that she was grateful . . . truly grateful.

She'd do whatever she could . . . no, whatever she HAD TO to free him.

. . . .

Dorothy eased back to the fringe of the camp and watched through the branches of a large bush. The creatures crawled back down the trees and gathered around Baltar, Saltooth and the boy.

Baltar began pleading with the tall one. "Give us just a little more time. She'll come, I tell you."

"Your time's up!" He pointed his knife to one of the others. "Get the boy!"

The creature stepped forward and took the rope from Saltooth.

"My stomach turns at the thought of eating Clutchboggin," the tall one said. "Stake them to the ground. Stretch them out. We'll leave'em for the mute woman. Once she's cut their tongues out, the wolves or the constrictors will do the rest."

They shoved the Clutchboggins to the ground and bound them as the tall one had commanded.

"Alright, let's go," the tall one said and started walking. The others followed.

Saltooth turned to Baltar. "I've heard she can make fire come out of her mouth."

Baltar pulled and struggled against the ropes that bound his arms and legs, unresponsive to Saltooth's comment.

"And, if your tongue is short," Saltooth added. "She'll pluck out your eyes to make up for it."

Baltar paused from straining at the ropes. He exhaled and looked at Saltooth. "Just laying there talking about it isn't helping anything. Try to get yourself free."

Dorothy broke off a limb from a bush as she walked into the clearing.

Baltar lifted his head. "You!"

Dorothy walked over and stood above him.

"If you'd been here five minutes ago, we wouldn't be in this situation and you'd have your friend back."

Dorothy reached down and took the pocketknife from his leather wristband. "You're a terrible liar." She started walking away.

The desperate Clutchboggins looked at each other. "Wait! Where are you going? Surely we can work something out," Baltar said.

"Don't just leave us here," Saltooth said.

Dorothy stopped and grinned. "Why? Do you have a deal in mind?"

"If you untie us, we'll help you get your friend back," Baltar said. "Treetrolls took him. We know where they're going."

"That's right," Saltooth said. "We do."

Dorothy reached down, picked up the piece of wood and put it in her pocket. She turned around and walked over to the dead Treetroll.

"Oh yeah," she said, keeping her back to them to appear apathetic. "And how do I know you're telling the truth?"

"I give you my word," Baltar said.

Dorothy bent down. "Your word? Really?" She bent down and took the Treetroll's knife from the corpse.

"I know. You have reason to be suspicious, but I assure you—"

Dorothy stood up. "Well, let me assure you of something." She turned and walked slowly to Baltar. She leaned down and leered at him. "Endora is my guardian. She's out there watching over me as we speak." Dorothy lifted her eyes and looked around, then back down at Baltar. "Anyone who harms me is her mortal enemy. You'd better keep that in mind. If you double cross me, she'll be on both of you before you can blink an eye. You got that?"

"Oh yeah, we got it!" Baltar looked at Saltooth. "Right, Saltooth?"

"Yeah. We got it. The last thing we want to do is get sideways with Endora."

Dorothy put the knife blade to Baltar's throat, her heart thumping in her chest. "Very well then. And there's one more thing."

Baltar swallowed a hard lump.

"Whatever you say."

"Being the liar you are, you may think I'm lying. So, ask yourself, 'How would she have that if Endora hadn't given it to her?'" She pulled the silver spoon out of her dress pocket and held it before his eyes. She pressed the point of the knife hard against his neck.

Baltar's eyes bulged. "Honestly . . . I never thought you'd come back with it."

Dorothy gazed at him with the coolness of a judge handing down a sentence. "Well, since we understand each other, I say we got ourselves a deal."

She returned the spoon to her pocket and cut Baltar free.

Chapter Twenty-One

From a distant rock ledge, Dorothy and the Clutchboggins spied down on the treetops. Cane domiciles with thatch roofs filled the limbs like apples ready to be picked at harvest time.

"That's where we'll find the boy," Saltooth said.

"How many of them do you think there are?" Dorothy said.

Baltar studied the situation. "Close to a hundred, I'd say. Maybe more."

Dorothy pushed back from the ledge and pulled herself into a sitting position. The Clutchboggins following suit.

"How many of you Clutchboggins are there?"

Baltar and Saltooth exchanged confused looks.

"Ah . . . two," Baltar said.

Oh brother. Surely Clutchboggins were not SO dense.

"No. I can see that. I mean all of you." Dorothy made a rolling motion with one hand. "You know, your whole clan or whatever you call yourselves."

"In all one hundred and seventy-three," Saltooth said. "Counting her-things and little-things."

"How many can wield a sword?"

Baltar rolled his eyes upward and rubbed his chin with one of his four palms. "In all I'd say about seventy. Sixty-eight."

"We'll need all of them. How long will it take you to go get them?"

The two Clutchboggins looked at each other again, sighed and looked down.

Dorothy cocked her head and looked at them. "They will help us, won't they? I did save the lives of two of their kin, you know."

A long pause. Dorothy wondered why the Clutchboggins didn't say anything.

"Well, don't just sit there, say something. His life's at stake."

Saltooth raised his eyes slowly to Baltar. "Are you gonna tell her or do you want me to?"

Baltar slumped his shoulders and shook his head. "I'll tell her." He exhaled as if he were about to get something heavy off his chest. "We can't ask them for help."

Dorothy lifted her hands in frustration. "Well, why not? Are they a bunch of cowards or what?"

Saltooth shook his head. "No. That's not it."

"Well, what's the problem? We're wasting time."

"We can't go to back our village," Baltar said. "We've been banished."

Saltooth nodded. "That's right. Ostracized. Shunned. At least for the time being."

"Why?"

Baltar struggled at an answer. "Because . . . because."

Saltooth turned his four palms up and tilted his head. "I'll tell her."

He looked to Dorothy. "We can't go back until we can produce something that shows we're brave."

"Brave? What do you mean?"

"Every Clutchboggin, on his birthday following the eighteenth double moon of his life, is sent out from the village. It's his mission. His quest . . . so to speak. He must do something daring and bring back something as a testimony."

"Like what?"

"My brother brought back a goblin's wand," Saltooth said. "And my father took off both the heads of a biserpent."

Baltar brought one of his hands to his chest. "My father stole the collar off one of the canines of the Kroll ruins." He extended the hand a bit, his palm turned upward, his eyebrows peaked. "And his father tamed one of the horned steeds of Basemath Valley."

"You see," Saltooth said. "We were never going to harm you or the boy. We fully intended to let you go free, but the Treetrolls bushwhacked us and took the boy."

"So, that's what trading for the pocket watch and the silver spoon was about?" Dorothy asked.

Baltar dropped his four hands to his sides. "Yes, If we would've returned with them, we would've been legends. We could've told our village that we took them from the Nesterclop and Endora. Just the mention of Endora's name strikes fear in every Clutchboggin"

"And, what about the pocketknife?"

Baltar pressed his lips. "Hmm. Pocketknife, huh. So that's what it's called,"

Dorothy stood to her feet. "Yes. It's not called a folding sword."

Baltar shrugged his shoulders. "I planned on keeping it. Never seen anything like it. A crown on one side. An owl on the other."

Dorothy sighed and put her hands on her hips. "Unbelievable. You both really had me convinced."

The two Clutchboggins stood up. Saltooth brought two of his hands to his chest. "We're Clutchboggins. Skilled in the art of dickering and flim-flam."

Baltar touched Dorothy on the elbow. "All our talk back there was just fog and smoke. We're not violent or cruel. We'll fight if we have to, but we'd rather trade our way out of a conflict."

"Trade, huh." Dorothy began pacing back and forth in front of them. "A trade . . . a trade . . . yeah. Well, maybe we can do just that."

"What do you have in mind?" Baltar said.

"I'll tell you on the way. Let's get going."

· ·

Baltar walked into the settlement, his shoulders back, his expression as cold as a stone. Treetrolls descended the tree trunks like an army of ants. The boy stood tied to a pole a short distance from an iron pot. Steam ascended from the pot as the fire under it crackled and roared.

The tall Treetroll, accompanied by his familiar band, stepped quickly toward the Clutchboggin, his knife drawn, the grin on his face displaying his devilish collection of jagged teeth. "Today is your day of death . . . a protracted, painful death."

Baltar marched forward and stopped in the middle of the camp, saying nothing, showing no sign of concern.

The tall one stepped close to him, flanked by his counterparts. He leaned in close to the Clutchboggin. "What a fool you are! Coming here!"

Baltar returned a cool expression. "Are you the highest rank among the Treetrolls?"

"I'm the highest rank you'll see before losing your head."

Baltar maintained his composure. "Your insults mean nothing to us. Besides, they waste our time and delay your possible good fortune."

"How's that?"

"Because I have come with a proposition that will render the Treetrolls untold riches. But I will speak to the highest rank and only to the highest rank."

"I'm the highest rank," a voice said.

The crowd parted like a torn cloth. The tall one turned and snapped to attention. A fanged Treetroll stood in the clearing between the two groups of his subjects. Upon his brow, just above his spiraled horn, sat a crown made of tree bark. A rough, green jewel lodged securely in the center of it. He started walking toward Baltar.

The tall one cut a look to Baltar. "You should bow."

Baltar turned to the tall one. He shook his head. "I bow to no one." He refocused his attention on the crowned leader.

As the leader came closer, Baltar folded his arms over his torso and continued staring him in the eyes. "I have something to offer you more valuable even than the crown that authenticates your rule," he said.

The tall one raised his knife. "Shall I cut his throat, my lord?"

The king raised his hand.

"No. I'm keen to hearing the Clutchboggin's proposition. It must be worthwhile or he'd never chanced walking into our domain." He motioned to Baltar. "Talk."

"I desire the prisoner you have in your possession."

"I figured that," the king said.

"He holds the heart of the Gem-fairy princess," Balta said. "Their love, though forbidden, is unbreakable. I serve at her command. I've been sent to inform you that, in exchange for him, she is prepared to give her most prized earthly possession. The very heartstone ring she wears."

"Ah!" went up in unison from the on looking Treetrolls followed by whispering conversations. The king shot his head back, a look of astonishment on his face. He raised his hand again to hush the crowd.

"My, my, my. You have not disappointed."

"So, do you agree to the trade?"

The king returned a slight grin. "Not so fast. First, you must prove your proposition."

Baltar turned and looked back.

"Your majesty! Show yourself!" he called out.

Dorothy stepped from behind a distant tree. She raised her hand toward the sun. The stone of the majestic ring caught the rays. It gleamed and sparkled before the Treetrolls. Another "Ah" ascended from the repulsive onlookers. Dorothy rotated and turned the ring, causing it to flash and glisten.

Behind the crowd, Saltooth hid in the woods on the edge of the Treetroll village, Linmar on the ground next to him. Saltooth opened the pocketknife and held it before the chipmunk. Linmar clenched the knife in his teeth and scurried to the boy.

The mesmerized Treetrolls continued to gaze at the ring's brilliant light display as if under a spell.

Linmar reached the boy and stood on his hind legs before him, the knife gripped tightly in his tiny jaws. The boy looked down and smiled. Linmar raced up one of the boy's pant legs. He climbed to the boy's bound hands and released the pocketknife. The boy sawed away at the rope, Linmar providing additional gnawing reinforcement. When his hands broke free, he cut the rope that bound his feet. Linmar led the way as he and the boy raced back to Saltooth.

Baltar glanced over to see the empty pole where the boy had been tied. He crossed his four hands behind his back, signaling to Dorothy that the boy was free. She returned the ring to her pocket and stepped back behind the tree.

Baltar gave the king a cool look. "So, do we have a deal?"

"We have a deal," the king said with glee. He turned to the tall one. "Release the prisoner and bring him to me."

The tall one walked to edge of the crowd and singled out one of his troops. "Release him and bring him here."

The Treetroll cut through the crowd in the direction where the boy had been.

Baltar waited, anticipating the best time to break and run.

"The boy has escaped!" the Treetroll shouted.

The tall one turned to the king. "It's a trick, my lord."

Baltar bolted.

"Take ten and pursue the boy," the tall one commanded a subordinate.

"Take ten and pursue the princess," he commanded another.

Without delay, each of the two struck out in a pursuit, his band of ten following. All with knives drawn.

The tall one turned back to the king. "My lord, shall I pursue the Clutchboggin?"

"Yes! And I want him alive!"

"Yes, my lord."

The tall one turned to the remaining Treetrolls. "Ten of you come with me. The rest of you stay here with the king."

. . . .

Dorothy was the first to arrive back at the checkpoint. The corpse was gone. A pool of thick dark blood marked the place where the tall one had slain the underling Treetroll earlier.

Dorothy sat on the trunk of a downed tree. She reached into her pocket and pulled out the block of wood. She studied it. What was the smooth, oddly shaped thing-a-majig? A crown etched on one side, an owl on the other. Something made a rustling sound. Dorothy shoved the carving back into her pocket and jumped from her seat. Standing on the balls of her feet she peered in direction of the commotion, her heart pumping. The sound grew louder. Closer. Dorothy gnawed her bottom lip, praying he'd emerge at any moment. The limbs of a hefty bush parted. Dorothy's high anticipation dropped like a brick.

Baltar stepped from the bush and into the clearing.

"Did you see the boy?" Dorothy asked.

"No. But he and Saltooth can't be far behind. Unless—" he caught himself and changed his sentence. "Unless they stopped on the way for a breather."

Dorothy knew that he almost said. *Unless the Treetrolls caught them.*

"You were really something back there. You had those Treetrolls all but hypnotized with that ring. I'm anxious to know. How'd you get it in the first place? One rarely sees a Gem-fairy. And for you to have the ring of the princess, there has to be a story—I mean a REAL story."

Baltar's comments cooled the blood in Dorothy's veins. The hazards and demands of her quest to break the Nesterclop's curse and the race against time to get back to free the Round-eyes had buried the hauntings of her dreadful deed. But now, with a few brief remarks, Baltar had opened a closed door and resurrected a torturous memory. And with it, guilt . . . deep guilt.

Baltar pressed the issue. "Well, tell me. Must have been some kind of adventure."

Dorothy inhaled and exhaled. "Oh, it's nothing of the sort. I used to be the most—"

The arrival of Saltooth and Linmar stole the rest of her sentence— saved her from making her tormenting re-confession. Linmar darted across the bare ground and stopped at her feet.

"*Eee. Eee,*" he squeaked, standing on his hind legs.

Dorothy reached down and her loyal friend climbed into her hand. She returned him to her pocket.

Dorothy looked at Saltooth. "Where's the boy?'

"He didn't—"

Dorothy interrupted, her voice fretful. "Make it? He didn't make it?"

Saltooth fanned his four palms. "No, that's not it. He made it. But he didn't come with me. Said he had something else that required his time."

Dorothy raised her hands in exasperation and clapped them down on her thighs. "He was going to help me deliver the Round-eyes! And, now he's decided to go do something else! Ugh! I can't believe it!" She clinched her fists at her sides. "That boy and his appointments! I just don't understand him sometimes!"

Baltar took a step toward her. "You've got us. We'll help you."

Saltooth stepped up next to him. "We certainly will. Come what may."

Dorothy shook her head and sighed. "Just the three of us? We wouldn't stand a chance."

"Now, think about it," Baltar said. "Just the three of us outsmarted the Treetrolls. I'm sure the three of us will figure out someway to deliver the Round-eyes."

Linmar raised his head and looked over the top of Dorothy's pocket. "Eek. Eek."

Saltooth grinned. "You mean four."

Chapter Twenty-Two

Dorothy and the Clutchboggins pulled themselves up to the edge of the cliff and looked down at the dry river bottom. Round-eyes carried buckets and pushed and pulled carts as Narrow-eyes lorded over them.

"Pick them up, you fool!" a Narrow-eye commanded and cracked his whip against a Round-eye's back.

The Round-eye winced in pain as he returned the wooden trolley back to its upright position. He began reloading the spilled rocks, a thick red line left on his back from the lash.

"Those Narrow-eyes certainly are brutal creatures," Baltar said.

"It wasn't always like this," Dorothy said. "It's because of the Nesterclop's curse. I tried to break it, but I failed. So, I purpose to do the next best thing. Free the Round-eyes."

Saltooth shook his head. "And I thought Snoglobbers were harsh."

"Wait till you see what Treetrolls can do!"

The familiar, gruesome voice hit them like clubs. Dorothy and the Clutchboggins reflexed and looked up to see the tall one and more than two-dozen Treetrolls standing behind him.

Dorothy jumped to her feet. "How did you—?"

The tall one didn't wait for her to finish the question. "The smell." He sniffed the air twice. "It's easy to track a Clutchboggin." He held out a gnarly hand and motioned with his three taloned fingers. "Give me the jewel."

Dorothy pulled down her brow and tightened her eyes. "I don't know what you're talking about."

The tall one grabbed up Saltooth and put his knife to the Clutchboggin's throat. "Give it to me or I'll cut him from ear to ear!"

Saltooth's feet dangled as he trembled in the tall one's grip.

Dorothy relaxed her face and slowly pulled the ring from her pocket. She began easing the ring toward his palm. She pulled her hand back quickly and held the ring over the side of the cliff.

"You listen to me. There's more than two hundred Crag Lurchers down there. You and your cronies are no match for them. They're as fierce as you are. Besides, I'm sure they'd love to have this as much as you would. Let him go or I'll drop it."

The tall one hesitated. Dorothy shook the ring in the air, daring him.

"Very well." The tall one released Saltooth. He held out his hand and Dorothy tossed him the ring. Saltooth rubbed his throat to remove the discomfort caused by the tall one's hold.

The tall one studied the dazzling ring, then shoved in into his waist pouch.

"Bind them and let's get going. It's a long walk back."

Dorothy shot him a cool look then cracked a slight grin. "He told you to bring us back alive, didn't he?"

"What are you talking about?"

"Your king . . . he told you to bring us back alive. You can't kill us."

He drew his blade from his scabbard and showed his gruesome teeth. "Keep it up, you little trixie and your clever tongue will get you the blade of my knife."

Dorothy rolled her eyes and sneered at him. "You're bluffing. If you were allowed to kill us, you would have the moment you acquired the ring." Dorothy nudged Baltar and Saltooth. "Don't be scared of him. He's just a puppet."

The tall one looked at her, his face revealing the fact that she'd called his bluff. "We're wasting time talking." He shoved his knife back in its sheath and turned to his followers. "Bind them and let's get a move on. This gorge and what goes on in it is of no concerns to us." He looked back at Dorothy, curled one side of his mouth then headed down the side of the hill.

Five Treetrolls stepped from the posse. They tied Dorothy and the Clutchboggins' hands then shoved them to start them on the descent.

As Dorothy moved down the embankment she pondered the Round-eyes' burdensome future. They would not be delivered from the heavy hand of the Narrow-eyes. She'd failed once again.

At the foot of the hills, the landscape flattened out. Open meadow gave way to thick forest. The tall one and his minions took to the road that cut through the woods.

Up ahead, a figure, clothed in a black cloak, sat at the edge of a tree by the road, the hood of his garment leaning downward over his knees.

A Treetroll looked up at the tall one. "Who do you think the sleeper is?" he said.

The tall one kept his eyes fixed ahead. "A fool who wishes to be robbed or killed. We'll gladly oblige him with both. Be ready."

When the Treetrolls drew close, the black-clad stranger raised his head and stood to his feet. He stepped into the middle of the road, his shoulders back, a ghoulish mask covering his face.

The tall one halted in the middle of the road and raised a hand, commanding his soldiers to do the same. "And just who might you be?" he said to the stranger.

"It matters not who I am," the stranger said calmly. "What matters is what I demand."

The tall one scoffed at the stranger. He twisted his head to the left then to the right, cracking the bones in his neck. "Demand? Are you blind as well as brainless?"

The troop of Treetrolls fanned out on each side of the stranger. Dorothy and the Clutchboggins stood by, waiting to see what would transpire.

"Who do you think that is?" Saltooth asked.

"I have no idea," Baltar said. "But I doubt he'll make it home for supper."

The stranger took a few steps toward the tall one. "I'm neither blind nor brainless. And if you and your subordinates hope to keep your heads on your shoulders, you'll submit to my demand."

One of the Treetrolls looked at the tall one. "Why don't you just let me gut'im and be done with it?"

The tall one raised his hand slightly. "No, no. Let's play along. The more he talks, the slower I'll kill him."

He turned his attention back to the stranger. "And just what exactly do you demand?"

"I'll have your prisoners and you'll have your lives. It's that simple."

The tall one raised his hand toward Dorothy and the Clutchboggins. "And just why, might I ask, do you want these two Clutchboggins and this . . . this female whatever she is?"

"My motivations should not concern you. Instead, your concern should be for your own life and the lives of your followers."

The tall one laughed scornfully. "We outnumber you thirty to one."

"I count thirty-three to be exact," the stranger said. "That is, as the eye can see. You're beginning to try my patience. I'll not demand a second time."

The tall one reached for his knife. "And, I'll not wait any longer to cut out your heart."

Before he could pull it, a bola wrapped around him, tethering his arms to his sides.

"If your go-fers even as much as reach fer their knives, the next one'll be round yer neck. You can tell yer granny that!"

"Sput!" Dorothy shouted and looked up to see him standing on a fallen log. Twenty Gnomes stepped out from behind trees, twirling bolas over their heads.

"And then your bodies will feel the pain of our stingers," came a piercing female voice from a different direction. Dorothy turned. The queen bee hovered. Her swarm rose up behind her.

"And then you'll perish from the points of our arrows," a noble looking being said. He was mounted on a steed and flanked by fifty others of his kind.

Baltar turned to Dorothy. "It's the Gem-fairy king.

"But not before I cut out your tongues and give them to her," the stranger said and pointed to a woman who stood on a boulder, holding a spear in one hand, a knife in the other.

"Endora!" Dorothy said.

Saltooth swallowed hard. "She gives me the gilly gobbies."

Dorothy wrinkled her brow and shook her head. "Oh, don't worry. Any friend of mine is a friend of hers."

The tall one relaxed his hand and dropped it to his side. "We'll do as you say." He turned to the three Treetrolls who held Dorothy and the Clutchboggins. "Release them."

The Treetrolls cut the ropes that bound Dorothy and the two Clutchboggins. Dorothy pulled her hands free and massaged her wrists.

"Okay. You have them now," the tall one said. "Will you unwrap this ball and leather weapon and let us be on our way?"

The stranger motioned to Sput. The witty Gnome jumped down from the log and walked up to the Treetroll leader. He put his thumbs under his suspenders and looked up at the tall one. "It's a powerful stranglehold. Wouldn't you say?"

"Just get me out of this!"

Sput grinned. "I'll take that as a yes," Sput started unwinding the bola.

The tall one turned his attention to the stranger. "Are we finished here?"

"Not just yet," Dorothy said and walked up to the tall one. She reached out her hand. "Give it here."

The tall one's countence turned submissive. He looked down at Dorothy's palm then up to the stranger. "But it wasn't part of the deal."

An arrow whisked through the air and pierced him just under his chin. He grabbed at his throat, his ghastly tongue protruding. Gurgling, he dropped to his knees.

"Neither was it part of the deal that I let you live," the Gem-fairy king said.

The tall one looked at him. His eyes rolled back in his head. Like a sawed tree, he fell face down to the ground. The impact drove the shaft of the arrow through the back of his neck. He jerked in his own blood as he expired. Dorothy rolled him over with her foot and recovered the ring from his leather pouch. With their mightiest warrior now vanquished, the Treetrolls raised their hands in frightful surrender.

"Please, sir. Give us our lives," one said to the stranger.

The stranger waved a hand. "Be gone."

The Treetrolls scattered as if fleeing a plague.

Dorothy walked over to the Gem-fairy king. She lifted the ring to him, her eyes filled with tears. "This belonged to your daughter."

The king looked down at her from his mount. "Yes, it did. Her mother gave it to her. As did her mother before her. It has been passed from generation to generation going all the way back to the first Gem-fairy queen."

He reached down and took the ring.

"Once, it was in my power to save your daughter's life," Dorothy said. "But with cunning and wickedness, I stole it and left her to die. So, you see, I'm as guilty as if I'd murdered her outright. It is one of the great regrets of my life. I certainly don't deserve what I am about to ask of you. In fact, I deserve to be shot through with one of your arrows just like the Treetroll. But I beg you, could you ever find it in your heart to forgive me?"

Dorothy fell to her knees. She held the stirruped foot of the Gem-fairy king and bowed her head. "Forgive me. Forgive me. I beg you. Forgive me," she pleaded, weeping all the while.

Dorothy felt a gentle hand on her shoulder.

"Rise and be not saddened," came a female voice. "Be relieved of this heavy burden."

Dorothy looked up into the smiling face of the princess.

"See, I am still alive."

Dorothy stood to her feet, her eyes wide open in astonishment.

"But how? I left you alone in the bog. The mud was at your chin. I saw it myself."

"You did leave me. But when you walked away, a deliverer came. He reached a saving hand to me and lifted me out of the pit. Because of him, I live and because of him, my father can forgive you."

Dorothy looked up at the king. "Is it true? Do you really forgive me?"

The Gem-fairy king gave an affirming nod, a gracious smile on his face. "I do indeed."

Dorothy turned her attention back to the princess. "But who? Who was this marvelous deliverer?"

"You are standing in his presence."

Dorothy looked at Sput. "Sput, was it you?"

"Tweren't me, Kansas."

She looked at the Clutchboggins. "Baltar . . . Saltooth? Was it one of you?"

They shook their heads.

"It was me," the stranger replied and pushed away his mask.

Thick, blonde hair trimmed his smiling face, his blue eyes gleaming with warm affection. The boy.

Dorothy lunged to him and embraced him.

"You're the greatest friend I've ever had. The greatest friend anyone could ever have for that matter."

The boy wrapped his arms around her and clapped her gently on the back.

"Dorothy, you have proven yourself to be a magnanimous friend as well." He tenderly pushed free of her embrace. "Now, stand by and see the benefit of what you have become."

The Guardian Owl flew down from a high tree. Just before he landed on the ground, rays of light shown around him as he transformed. First into the man who counseled her to have faith. Then into the Wearer of the White Crown.

"Dorothy," he said, "You are not the same girl as you were at our first encounter. Your journey on the Red Brick Road has altered you and enabled you to alter the lives of others. When you rescued the Hunchback, he was able to return to the cave at Rantoul Grove. You, Dorothy, restored that which was once lost. And, when you visited Endora in the swamp, you demonstrated courageous benevolence as none before you had ever done. You showed love to one who was unlovely."

Dorothy looked over at Endora.

"Thank you," Endora mouthed and brought a hand to her heart.

"Then, when you lifted the princess's ring to the Gem-fairy king and begged for his forgiveness you demonstrated genuine, heartfelt repentance for a wrong suffered. Therefore, the curse shall be broken and the people of the Red Brick Road can live in the fellowship and harmony of the former days before the Nesterclop came."

Upon saying this, the Wearer of the White Crown raised both of his hands. "So, let it be done!" He ascended high above the trees of the forest.

He looked down at Dorothy and extended a hand. "Come. See the great good you have secured."

Dorothy rose up to meet him in the air. With the whole of the landscape of the Red Brick Road in view, Dorothy watched as the Wearer of the White Crown began reviving the land. He pointed to the gorge and the Narrow-eyes became Round-eyes again. And with their transformation, they threw down their whips and humbled themselves before the other Round-eyes. Egscar hugged Nargoul, Houstess and Harlice. Monguzi ran from his lair and fell on his face before the one he'd wronged so greatly. In response, Zimboza raised up the once brutal Crag Lurcher and embraced him with brotherly affection. The Wearer of the White Crown pointed to the Prison of Keylon. The bars raised and Benellus stepped forth. The Wearer of the White Crown then snapped his fingers and Benellus was transported to the gorge as if carried by an invisible chariot. The Crag Lurchers shouted and rejoiced as they stood in line to greet their true leader.

The Wearer of the White Crown pointed to Rantoul Grove and water burst forth from the Hunchback's cave. The water traveled throughout the land, filling the formerly dry river and creek beds. As it went forth, flowers bloomed, fruit trees blossomed and wildlife frolicked in the waters and along the banks.

Next, the Wearer of the White Crown pointed to the Tree of Pulaski. The great tree uprooted from the ground and rocketed to a broad meadow close to the gorge. The tree grew to twice its size and the legendary honeybees swarmed to its lofty boughs and vibrant leaves and blossoms.

Then, the powerful sage turned his attention to a region of the land unfamiliar to Dorothy. A region populated with numerous dome dwellings. He snapped his fingers and all the Clutchboggins came out of the domes and assembled themselves in a single-file line. The Wearer of the White Crown pointed toward the gorge and the Clutchboggins began marching.

The Wearer of the White Crown turned to the land of the Gnomes. He clapped his hands and a shower of stars sprinkled their forest. The Gnomes paraded from the trees singing and celebrating. The Wearer of the White Crown cupped a hand. He motioned it toward the now flowing gorge and Sput's relatives were transported to the land of the Crag Lurchers. Dorothy looked on as the former foes reconciled with glee and enthusiasm.

"And finally, the land shall be cleansed of the disgraceful," the Wearer of the White Crown said and grasped into the air. He raised his fists as if uprooting weeds. When he did, he plucked Scaithes from their hiding caves, the Molewiggins from Darckbaal Mountain and the Treetrolls from their loathsome village. The Wearer of the White Crown made a flinging motion toward the Devil's Spit Spot and the black lake sucked in the entire collection of ghastly, detestable creatures.

"Alas, O land, be fruitful and bless these your citizens. And all creatures, both great and small, live in the bounty and the blessing for which you were created. It is finished."

And with that, he and Dorothy descended back down to the Gnomes, the Clutchboggins, the Gem-fairies, Endora, and the boy.

The Wearer of the White Crown lifted his voice and proclaimed, "All of you! Make your way to the great gorge! Your fellow countrymen await you! Today is a new day. Let there be feasting and dancing and singing for that which was all but dead has come back to life!"

"But wait!" Dorothy interjected. "Might I ask just one thing?"

The Wearer of the White Crown looked down at her. "Certainly. Ask me whatever you wish."

"Might I get my Toto back? Oh, how I do miss him."

The Wearer of the White Crown turned to the boy. "That's a matter I'll leave to you."

The boy nodded. "Very well." He looked at Dorothy and gave a tight smile. "I think you have a piece of wood in your pocket. Do you not?"

"Yes, I do," Dorothy said and reached into her pocket. "I've been meaning to give it back to you." She pulled it out and offered it to the boy.

"Look at it. What do you think it is?"

Dorothy turned it over in her hand, inspecting it. "I'm not sure. It looks like a whistle or something."

The boy winked. "A whistle it is."

Dorothy continued to study it.

"Well, go ahead," he said. "Blow it and see what happens."

Dorothy placed the whistle between her lips and blew. A high-pitched sound resonated throughout the forest. Linmar emerged from her dress pocket and jumped to the ground. Rays of light radiated from the resourceful chipmunk and he was transfigured into Toto before Dorothy's eyes.

He barked and stood up on his hind legs.

Dorothy reached down and picked him up. He began licking her face profusely. "So, you were with me all the time?"

"Yes, he was with you all the time," the boy said.

Dorothy sat Toto back down on the ground and looked into the boy's eyes. "By the way, you know my name, but I don't know yours."

The boy smiled. "Rikkan. My name is Rikkan."

"Now that all is settled," the Wearer of the White Crown said. "I'm sure you'd like to be on your way to the Wizard of Oz . . . that is, unless you'd like to help us celebrate before you go."

Dorothy looked around at their smiling, encouraging faces then back at the Wearer of the White Crown. "I suppose it would be rude to leave without saying goodbye to Nargoul, Houstess and Harlice."

And so, the land of the Red Brick Road was once again as it once was. All its citizens. From the Crag Lurchers to the Gem-fairies. From the Gnomes to the Clutchboggins to the Hunchback. As well as its creatures. From the bighorn sheep that walk on their hind legs and have hands like monkeys to the giant red tortoises that have blue wings with white polka dots. All were transformed back into perfect harmony. At the command of the Wearer of the White Crown, they all made their way to the gorge. And, when they arrived, they commenced a celebration, the likes of which had never been seen before in all the land of the Red Brick Road. And you can tell yer granny that.

The End

Made in the USA
Middletown, DE
23 October 2022

13326259R00168